ROBYN'S T...
Part 1 – Seduced Int

CW00428909

Peter King

ROBYN'S TALE
Part 1 – Seduced Into Submission

SILVER MOON BOOKS

INTRODUCTION

Robyn Milford was a rambunctious girl, so much so that her parents sent her to a private school for the children of the wealthy that had social issues. While they kept her worst instincts in check, mostly, they did nothing to quell her rebellious nature. Truth be told, the school was glad when she graduated just after her eighteenth birthday and she went home. Since both her parents were summering in France, Robyn returned to their house with just the servants in residence.

Robyn was always a cute girl, but in the last year or so, her body began maturing and she started looking more like a woman. She had curly auburn hair and bright green eyes with just a hint of freckles peppering her alabaster skin. She was five and a half feet tall and weighed just under a hundred and twenty pounds on her eighteenth birthday. Her body was becoming curvaceous too, as her hips measured thirty four inches with a twenty four inch waist. But it was her breasts that grew the most in the last year, going from nearly a meager 32B to a 36C cup.

Now out of high school, and with no plans for college, Robyn planned on having a fun filled summer. But after being home just a few days Robyn noticed they had a new neighbor, an extremely handsome man. Her parents' home, though very large, shared a cul-de-sac with two other spacious houses. They were separated by ample foliage and set back from the road, but they all had mailboxes at the ends of their driveways, and that was where she first saw her new neighbor.

One day, Robyn had gone out to the mailbox to get the mail when she saw him across the circular court at his mailbox. He had long blonde hair and was just wearing shorts and a tee shirt, so she could see how muscular he was. When he smiled and waved at her before heading back up his driveway, Robyn returned the gesture. But her smile was fueled by a strong desire to meet him. Though she had a relationship with a boy at school, Robyn had never gone all the way. But at her age, the desire to explore her sexuality was rapidly growing. Seeing such a sexy man living across the street triggered a new desire for her summer, getting to know him!

It took a few days of internet searches, but Robyn eventually discovered that his name was George Mayfield. He had created one of the most popular video games on the market, sold the rights to it, and retired in his twenties! He was not only rich; he was young and hot too! Robyn had no real ambitions to pursue further education, or heaven forbid, work for a living. Now that she knew that there was a man living just across the street that might be able to give her the kind of life she aspired to have, she decided that she had to find a way to meet him.

She began watching his house to look for a way to introduce herself to him, but there was a problem. There was a parade of hot women that came and went from his house. And never the same one twice, and only for a day or two at most. She was not surprised that he was able to attract sexy looking women, but she guessed that he had no steady partner. She also followed him a few times when he went out in his Porsche, but he went to clubs that she was not old enough to patronize. Then, fate gave her an in, when she found a piece of his mail mixed in with hers. It took her a few days to screw up her courage and figure out how to approach him before she decided to deliver it. Robyn had no idea what she was about to begin, or how it would change everything.

CHAPTER 1: MEETING HIM

Robyn spent hours trying to decide what to wear for her first meeting with George. She tried on sexy dresses, but decided she did not want to look too provocative. She eventually decided to go with skin tight leggings, a sports bra, and a somewhat loose tee shirt that was a bit long in the tail. She started to get ready when she knew he was alone, having seen his latest guest leave a few hours ago. She went with very little makeup, wanting to look like she was dressed for a jog or something like that, though she was not into exercising at all.

Having taken to spying on him with binoculars from a little niche in the hedges at the front of her parent's property, Robyn found a way to see all the way up the driveway to the front door of his house. On the day she planned to return his mail, she saw the latest guest of his come out of it after a car service pulled into the driveway. Usually, the women came out looking as impeccable as they did when they arrived, but this one looked a little disheveled. Some did, and Robyn always wondered why that was. As the car drove away, Robyn dashed back into the house to get dressed for her first encounter with George.

As she looked at her reflection in the mirror, Robyn thought she looked just right, not too blatantly suggestive, but definitely with a sexual undertone. Her shiny pink leggings and matching sneakers made her legs look great, and though the tee shirt was not skin tight, it did not hide her recently developed breasts. She figured he was at least a little bit of a nerd, given the fact that he created a video game, so the tee shirt she picked had the logo of his game on it. If he thought she was a fan of his game, Robyn hoped it would give him a reason to get to know her better. She had never played it before, but in the weeks she watched him before she found the excuse to meet him, she bought a copy and got very well acquainted with it.

She felt she was ready, even rehearsing what she would say when she was face to face with him. Shortly after seeing him retrieve his mail from his box, Robyn went across the court with his letter in hand. When she reached his front door Robyn felt extremely nervous, and not wanting to make a bad impression, she took a few breaths before ringing the doorbell. It took a few moments before it opened, and when she saw him, Robyn could feel her palms get all sweaty.

She could not even utter a word, but he just smiled and said, "Aren't you are the girl from across the street, the one I have seen getting the mail?"

"Yes…that's me," Robyn replied, but again was at a loss for what to say next.

"Well then, hello neighbor! I'm George, and who do I have the pleasure of meeting?"

"I'm Robyn…pleased to meet you too."

"So, what brings you over Robyn?"

Holding up the letter, she said, "This accidently ended up in our mailbox, I just wanted to bring it over and meet my new neighbor," she answered, hoping she didn't sound too nervous.

"You look a little young to own a home here, do you live with your parents?" he asked.

"Yes, I live in their house."

"Are they the older couple I have seen coming and going in the SUV?"

"No, my parents are in France for the summer, the ones you saw are their butler and cook."

"Would you like to come in for a drink and get to know each other, or do you have plans?" he asked in a friendly manner.

"Sure, I have some free time," she said, thinking she sounded stupid.

He waved her inside, and once he closed the door, he led her to his back patio by the pool. He held out a chair for her next to a round glass table, and once she was seated, he asked, "Would you like a soft drink, or something harder?"

"Oh, I'm not old enough to drink alcohol," she said, and as she did, she wished she had not admitted how young she was.

"No problem, what would you like?"

"Iced tea?" she ventured, her nerves now getting the best of her.

"Good, I will be right back," he said, and then he left to get it.

Robyn tried to calm herself, drying her palms on her tee shirt and hoping she would not sound like a smitten girl, even though she was. He was not only great looking and well- built, he sounded really nice and friendly too. In a couple of minutes, he returned with a glass for her and a bottle of beer for him, taking a seat across the table and taking a swig from the bottle.

Then he put the bottle down and said, "So tell me about Robyn, is she a gamer?" pointing at the logo on her shirt.

"I only started playing recently, after I graduated high school I had plenty of free time," she answered, as she wanted him to know she was not a kid anymore.

"Did you just graduate?"

"A month ago, just after I turned eighteen."

"Happy Birthday then! Old enough to vote, but not to drink, an adult in some ways, but not others. I remember it was an annoying time for me. Are you planning on going to college?"

"I don't know, I was going to take the summer to think about what to do next."

"It is always good to think about things before you make a decision. I bet you and your friends have lots of plans for the next few months."

"I just got back from boarding school, I don't have any friends around here," she said, trying to hint at her availability.

"Not even a boyfriend?"

"I kind of had one at school, but he is off to university this fall after vacationing with his parents in the Caribbean for the summer."

George was digesting what he heard, and could tell this girl was interested in him. He was only twenty seven, and even though he was not too much older than her, eighteen still seemed kind of young. But she was also a sexy looking redhead, and he always had a sweet spot for the Gingers. He was mostly satisfied with all the one night stands he was having, but he knew if he pursued this one, it would have to be something more. Having a fling with a neighbor could create problems.

"Well, I'm new to the area too, maybe we can do some things together this summer," he ventured, testing his belief that she was interested in him.

Robyn could not believe he just said that, and she quickly replied, "That sounds nice, I have been kind of bored since I got home."

"Would you like to go out to dinner with me tonight?" he asked, looking at her carefully as he did.

"I don't have any plans...so, sure," she answered, trying to contain her delight.

George saw right through it, knowing this girl was into him, he had seen that look after a proposition plenty of times. He had also seen her spying on him, and now he was pretty sure she had the hots for him. He still was not sure he wanted to go any farther, but he figured a nice dinner in a fancy restaurant would give him enough time to decide. His current string of short affairs was fine, but all the women he met were more enamored by his wealth than himself. This girl was from a wealthy family, obviously, so he was curious to see if this one might be different.

"What is your favorite food Robyn?" he asked.

"I love seafood, but any restaurant you choose would be fine," she answered eagerly.

"I know a great place that flies in fresh Maine lobsters every day, how does eight o'clock sound?" He said, seeing her get even more excited.

"That sounds great, is there a dress code?"

"Suit and tie for men, and if I have to dress up, I would hope you would wear a nice dress. Is that fair?" he asked, not wanting to blatantly tell her to doll herself up, even though he just did.

"I have some nice dresses that I don't wear often enough, so it is a deal," she replied.

"Great, I will make the reservation and pick you up at seven-thirty, does that sound good?"

"It sure does."

"Good, but if you don't mind, I have a few things to do before dinner. We can pick up the conversation later if that is alright with you."

"Oh OK, I need to do a few things myself," she said, as she saw him stand up and she followed suit. Once she was out of the house and walking back to hers, Robyn noticed how wet her crotch felt and how excited she was feeling.

She headed straight for the shower, running the water as she stripped. She blushed when she saw how soaked her panties were, it even seeped into the crotch of her leggings! That left her wondering if he had seen it! It was kind of humiliating, but also kind of naughty and exciting. She jumped into the shower and rubbed her sex until the orgasm that was simmering inside her boiled over, as she imagined doing *it* with him.

Robyn was not technically a virgin; she had a healthy dildo collection that she used often. She thought she had some real experience, as the guy she was with in school shared some very heavy petting together. She had even sucked his cock, and she let him lick her pussy, but they

14

never did *it*. Given George liked to entertain women at his house, as she saw plenty of them come, stay, and then go, so it seemed possible that he might make a pass at her. She kind of wanted him to and she was pretty sure she would be thrilled to have him be the first man she had real sex with.

She had two orgasms before she began washing herself, feeling much better about her prospects with this man. Now that the fire between her thighs was satiated, she began considering what to wear. It was an easy choice, her little black dress and matching pumps. Given that choice, she shaved her legs and trimmed around her sparse ginger colored bush. She considered going for the clean look, but if they did get naked, she wanted him to know she was a natural redhead.

She was in a strange state of mind, she had never been so fixated on someone the way she was with George. It was like an animal attraction, a drive to be completely intimate with him, despite the fact that she barely knew him. It was both troubling and arousing, and maybe dangerous too. He was almost ten years older than her, and he clearly had no issues getting beautiful women to sleep with him. That made her feel rather inadequate and she started to wonder if this wasn't just a pity date, having realized that she portrayed herself as a poor rich girl with no social life.

That added a hint of doubt into Robyn's mind, but she was determined to show him that she was not a girl, she was a woman. After a luxurious shower, she dried herself off before sitting naked at her vanity. She looked at her reflection, while arching her back to admire her newly sprouted breasts. It was not until after they started growing, along with the bush now framing her sex, that Robyn became rather obsessed with sex, masturbatory mainly.

Robyn also watched porn, quite a bit really, and that just added to her desire to try the real thing. The fact that she was so attracted to an older man like George was probably because she had found that she liked the sex videos of younger girls having rough sex with older men. She was not looking for romance or a relationship, she was just a horny girl. One that wanted a big strong man to have his way with her, any way he wanted. As headstrong as she was most of the time, she was hoping that George would sweep her off her feet. She knew very little about sex and wanted, no needed, an experienced man to show her how it should be done.

She dried her hair with a blow drier and just used a floral clip to gather it behind her neck. Then she applied enough makeup to make her green eyes sparkle, but not so much to make her look slutty. A little clear lip gloss, and no rouge, just a sweet looking natural girl, she thought. The dress would make the statement she wanted, her body looked sexy now and she knew it. She donned a strapless bra, since the dress only had thin spaghetti straps. She also put on a pair of sexy lace panties, but no stockings were needed, her freshly shaved legs looked superb.

Once she slipped on the skin tight dress, and smoothed it around her recently developed curves, she looked at her reflection in the dressing mirror. It made Robyn smile; she really did look hot. Even though it was a pretty revealing outfit, it was also rather popular with countless young ladies these days. Many of his visitors dressed much like this, and she hoped it would signal her strong desire to get much closer to him.

She was ready half an hour early, and the subsequent wait seemed like it took forever. She watched from an upstairs window that looked over the hedge to the street, and his driveway on the other side. When she saw his garage door opening, Robyn headed downstairs to the front door. By the time she got there she could see his car pulling into her driveway, but it stopped near the street and the horn blew once.

Robyn thought he was a bit rude doing that, but she also thought that she wanted a bad boy, and this was a sign he might actually be one. As she exited the house and walked down the path to the driveway, another thought crossed her mind, maybe he wanted to check her out in her outfit. She made sure to walk as steadily as she could in her heels, noting how it made her ass wiggle in a way it usually didn't. And her breasts were bouncing too with the exposed upper slopes of her exposed mounds jiggling like Jell-O.

Once Robyn was close to the Porsche, he surprised her by getting out to open the passenger side door for her. Once she got in, a tricky affair with such a short hem on her dress, he closed the door and went around to get back into the driver's seat. It gave her enough time to pull the bottom of her dress back down to mid-thigh, and buckle her seat belt. She became even more nervous when he clicked his seatbelt together.

"You look great in that dress Robyn," he said.

"Thanks, you look pretty good in a suit too," she answered, feeling good that he liked the way she was dressed.

The ride to the restaurant consisted of George asking Robyn questions, with her answering them. In less than half an hour he had a pretty good picture of the young lady. If he decided to pursue an actual relationship with her, there was no one around her that could cause him any issues. He had been waiting to find a particular type of partner for a relationship, and it was not the standard most people sought. The parade of women who came to visit him knew what he liked before he brought them home, and though they all played his game, none so far wanted to extend it beyond their singular encounter.

George was seeking a submissive woman to compliment his dominant nature, one that would enjoy the kinky games he liked to play. Though he gave all his guests a night they would never forget, as he was highly skilled at making women squeal in ecstasy, none wanted to take it to the level he spelled out after their first tryst. He was now thinking that this younger woman, all the others were at least in their twenties, might be more amenable to his desires.

Robyn was clearly smitten with him, and he quickly ascertained that she was also sexually naïve. Though she avoided details, he guessed that her high school boyfriend was more of a fling than a love affair. He believed that they were both just exploring the concept of intimacy with each other, and he doubted she even went all the way with him. If she had never had sex with him, then she was still basically a virgin. It might provide him the opportunity to show her the wild side of sex without preconceptions from other intimate encounters, like the other women he had been playing with up until now.

Their dinner was delicious, and though she drank no liquor to quell her inhibitions, he could tell she really wanted him to seduce her. He decided that he would test her sensibilities on the ride home, letting her know that getting involved with him had certain caveats. It would be a delicate kind of conversation, letting her know what he was looking for without scaring her away. But he was fairly certain that her seemingly adventurous spirit would give her the impetus to accept his proposal. Once they were in the car, and driving back home, he made his move.

CHAPTER 2: SPANKED!

As they pulled out of the restaurant parking lot, George asked, "Did you enjoy your dinner Robyn?"

"It was delicious and thank you for taking me out, it has been a while," she answered.

"A girl like you ought to go out more often, you are young and this is the time to enjoy yourself before real life intrudes." Then he completely changed the subject and said, "So, tell me Robyn, are you physically attracted to me?" even though he already knew the answer.

That question caught her off guard, it was far more forward than he had been so far. She tried to formulate an answer that said yes, but not so blatantly. So, she answered, "Well, I don't usually dress up like this, and I hoped you would notice it."

"A simple yes or no young lady, no more games," he said in a stern tone of voice.

"Yes, but…"

"No buts," he interrupted her, and then he said, "You are very young, legally an adult yes, but you are also very inexperienced. You just met me today, are you ready to take such a big risk, the kind that intimacy creates?"

"I don't know George, all I know is that I am attracted to you," she answered, as the doubts she was having returned from his sobering comment. This was not how it was supposed to go and she had no idea what he was doing.

"I know you have been watching me, and the variety of ladies that come by to visit me. I bet you are wondering why you never see the same woman twice."

Robyn was fully flustered at that point, and she blurted out, "I'm sorry, I was just curious," as she wondered if he was just going to dump her on her driveway.

"So, you admit to stalking me, tell me Robyn, what are your true intentions?"

"I...I...just wanted to get to know you," she said nervously.

"There are better ways to get to know someone than stalking them. I appreciate your desire to know me, but frankly young lady, you deserve to be punished for what you did."

Robyn was shocked and totally dejected, so she said, "You are right. You can drop me at home and I promise not to bother you again."

"And how does that make up for what you did?"

"I don't know, what are you suggesting?"

"Well, my guess is that you have gotten away with many other bad acts, and maybe this time you should pay a price for it."

"What does that mean?"

"For a girl like you? A good hard spanking would do you a world of good."

"A spanking? I'm not a child!"

"You sure sound like one, so I will give you a choice. When we get back, if you choose to come to my place I will give you that spanking, and after that, maybe you will get what you really want. Or, I will drop you at your

21

house and we can go our separate ways. Don't say a thing, just think about it, and when we get home, you can make your choice."

Robyn was in shock; his proposal was both chilling and enticing. She remembered the videos she watched with bratty teens teasing guys and then getting into trouble with them. A few of them did get spankings, and, as she thought about it, a tingle in her pussy gave her a strong incentive to accept his offer. Then there was the other part of his offer, about getting what she really wanted. She felt so overmatched, this man had her all figured out, and it was disturbing. But, despite his promise to spank her, her attraction to him seemed even stronger now. They were getting close to home and Robyn had no idea what to do, but she decided she had to say something.

She had remained quiet until they were nearly there, and then she said, "I don't want to be like the others, one and done. I have never been with a man before, and I don't want my first time to be a one night stand."

George was pleased that she ignored his request and also that she was actually considering his proposal. He did not fault her logic, but he also knew he might have something in this girl. His normal approach was to start vanilla and then turn kinky, but this one now knew he planned to spank her first and she was still thinking that she might accept his proposal. Since all the others had the chance to remain with him, but declined after a long and raucous night with him, he decided to tell Robyn even more about his preferences.

"Every one of the women you watched leaving my place could have come back, but even though they left sexually satisfied, they were not adventurous enough to continue. If you decide that you want me to discipline you, I am sure you will learn a lot. Then, if you want it to continue, I am sure we can make an arrangement."

"Adventurous enough? What does that mean?"

"I am looking for a woman who likes to play on the edge. I am not looking for a partner, I am seeking a woman who can accept a more structured and disciplined relationship."

Robyn was getting the hint, talking about spankings and discipline had to mean he wanted a woman who would like being treated like she belonged to him. She knew a little about it from her porn searches, he was looking for a specific type of girl. One that wanted a man to make all the decisions for her, but it was not something she ever considered for herself.

She knew the word, and she said, "You want a submissive woman."

"That is the starting point, and as you can guess, none of the ones you saw had that type of disposition. I don't expect you to know if you are one, but I can promise that we would find out if you spend the night with me."

"I don't want to be hurt," she said, not sure if she meant physically or mentally.

"The fact that you are considering my proposition is in conflict with what you just said, spankings always hurt. But, what I think you mean is you don't want to be damaged. If you do not like how you feel after your punishment, you will be free to go. If you do want to continue being with me, it will be your choice."

Robyn digested his statement, and the last part made it seem less frightening. But he was pretty clear about what he wanted from her and she was not at all sure that she was that kind of girl. But there was the little matter of her pussy, which had gotten all wet and tingly during this conversation. Even though she never thought about being submissive to a man, there was an air about George that made that idea seem kind of exciting. She saw that they were approaching the cul-de-sac and she knew she had to make a decision!

He stopped the car in the road, with her driveway to the right and his to the left. George said, "Time to make a choice, left or right. Which is it Robyn?"

She hesitated a moment, then quietly said, "Left."

"Good choice, now going forward you will call me Sir. Let me hear your answer again."

"Left please…Sir," she said louder, and saying those words sent a little thrill up her spine.

He turned the car onto his driveway and the drove into his garage. As the overhead door started to close, Robyn felt a strange feeling of entrapment. Not so much by him, but more like she was caught in a fantasy that she created. She had pursued him, and not even the parade of women that came and went from his place deterred her. She knew she was playing a risky game, and now she had agreed to be spanked by a man she just met earlier that day. She still had no idea why she agreed to this, only that her budding attraction to him was the catalyst that sparked this decision.

She watched him, as if in a trance, as he got out of the car and walked around to her door. He opened it and said, "Out you go girl." Robyn climbed out of the car and stood next to him as he closed the door, and then he said, "Follow me."

She followed him into the house through a door inside the garage, emerging in his kitchen. But he continued on, until they arrived in a room full of books on wall shelves with a fireplace on one wall. There was a leather wing back chair and a matching ottoman in front of the fireplace, and he walked over to it and sat down on the chair. She had followed him all the way, and she stood by the side of the chair once he was seated, not knowing what to do next.

"Stand in front of the fireplace and face me Robyn," he said, and she did.

"You have been a naughty girl Robyn, not only by spying on me, but basically lying to me when we met today. It was not about returning my mail; it was about getting my attention. Isn't that right Robyn?" he said sternly.

"Yes Sir," she said, feeling very small and petty.

"Tell me what you are Robyn."

"I am a naughty girl, Sir."

"And what happens to naughty girls?"

"They get punished."

"Do you need to be punished Robyn?"

"Yes Sir," she replied, as she realized this conversation was making her even hornier.

"Are you aroused too?"

"Yes Sir," she replied, in a whisper this time.

"What did you say?"

"YES SIR!" she shouted, and she felt her panties getting wetter as she did.

"Prove it, take off your panties and give them to me," he said flatly.

Robyn hesitated for a moment, but then said, "Yes Sir," as she reached behind her back and lifted the hem of the dress high enough to hook her thumbs under the waistband of her panties. The way she pulled them down kept her sex from his view when her panties fell to her ankles. She stepped out of one side with her left foot before lifting her right leg behind her so she could grab them without bending down and possibly flashing him. Then she handed them to him, blushing when she did.

He took them and opened them up to reveal the saturated gusset. Robyn felt humiliated and exposed like never before, and for some strange reason, her arousal was still escalating. She watched him sniff the moist crotch while smiling at her, making her feel even more uncomfortable. He was planning to spank her, and he knew she was already horny. She began to think that maybe she did want to submit to him, since she could not deny the sexual heat building up inside her.

"You may have what it takes girl, and your cunt smells delicious. But first things first, that cute little ass of yours needs a spanking." Then he slid to the edge of the chair so his knees stuck out in front of it, and said, "We will start with an old fashioned over the knee spanking. Get over here and bend over my legs."

"Yes Sir," she said rather breathlessly with both fear and excitement gripping her.

She moved over to his right side so her legs were next to his thighs, and she started to bend over, as she stuck her arm out to grab the armrest on his left side. But before she reached it, he grabbed her wrist and yanked it down in front of the chair so that she fell over his legs. It knocked the wind out of her, and as she was trying to regain her composure, he swung his right leg over her the backs of her thighs. He squeezed his legs together, trapping her thighs between his. She felt his left hand gripping the back of her neck and pushing her down toward the floor.

She yelped and started to struggle a little, and he said, "Calm down and relax girl, this spanking can be done the easy way or the hard way, your choice. But it is going to happen."

"Sorry Sir, you just surprised me, I will be good," she said, surprised that she really did want to be good for him.

"It won't be the last surprise girl. Now stay still and brace your upper body, I have your legs under control. Once I begin, you will say, 'Thank you Sir, may I have another?' after each slap until I decide to end it. Is that perfectly clear girl?"

"Yes Sir!" Robyn replied, as she bent far enough down so that her elbows and lower arms were resting on the floor. She had no idea what to expect, but what he wanted her to do made it sound so much sexier than just getting spanked. Thanking him after every blow sounded bizarre and demeaning, but also oddly alluring.

Once she had situated herself, he said, "The problem with you is that you are a child in a woman's body, one that desperately needs discipline. I can provide a path for you, but it will be nothing like what you ever imagined. Tonight, we will explore that possibility and find out if you will want to follow my lead."

Robyn heard him clearly, and wondered if he was right. She had always done what she wanted, and more often than not, it got her into trouble. Maybe she was a child, just acting out to get attention, and this time she got both his attention and the trouble that came along with it. He gave her the choice to walk away, and the fact that she was now bent over his knees, suggested that she did want him to curb her undisciplined nature. Those thoughts were interrupted when she felt him slide her dress up to expose her bare rump to his view, and it gave her another thrill.

Robyn felt even better when he said, "What a sweet little ass, and it will look even better once I add a little color to it."

Unable to resist the urge, Robyn said, "Yes Sir, thank you Sir."

He placed his left hand flat against the middle of her back, as he used his right one to knead her firm cheeks. Robyn both moaned and trembled from his touch, it was so sensual. She could barely breathe, knowing what was coming, but enjoying the way he was massaging her buttocks. She tensed up a little when his fingers slipped between the juncture of her thighs and caressed the wet lips of her pussy, making her shiver and moan again.

"You are such a horny little girl! We will see if you still are once you take your medicine," he said, and he followed it with a hard slap on her right buttock.

"AAAAH!" Robyn squealed from the unexpected blow, but then she cried out, "Thank you Sir! May I have another?"

As soon as he said, "Good girl." he added another slap to her left cheek.

She gave him the required reply, and then she moaned because he began massaging her sore rump again. She winced at first, as the slaps left her buns stinging, but his gentle massage felt even more exciting. He continued alternating slaps and massages, and her rump got hot and tender, but her pussy was literally on fire too. Getting spanked by him was the most erotic thing she ever experienced, the heavy petting sessions with her ex-boyfriend did not even come close.

He lectured her and she cried throughout the process. He took his time to make sure that, as the pain mounted, so did her arousal. He dipped his fingers between her thighs after every few slaps, and it was obvious that her sex was responding the way he wanted. But arousal from a palm spanking was not a real test, and he had other ways to learn if she was the kind of girl he was seeking. She was a sexy little minx, and the possibility of fully training her was tempting, but he needed to make sure she wanted the same thing he did first.

George did not count how many slaps he delivered, but he guessed maybe fifty or so, and he was impressed how she thanked him for every single one. Her voice had become raspy, and she shuddered from each blow after the first dozen or so, once her cheeks were properly tenderized. But she never struggled or asked him to stop, not to mention his pants were now soaked with her pussy juice. When he released his grip on her legs and back, George used both hands to roll her off his lap and onto her back on top of the ottoman.

Robyn winced when her bare butt touched the leather covering, but she was in a strange state of mind and she remained quiet. Her legs were askew, and she did not even notice how her ginger framed sex was now plainly in his view. She was trying to understand how her bottom could hurt so badly, while her sex was obviously ready to have an orgasm. And the last few swats on her ass might have put her over the top, but she actively resisted the urge let go, afraid of what it might mean if she actually climaxed from just a spanking.

"What do you have to say Robyn?" he asked, seeing the faraway look in her eyes.

Without a thought about it, she answered, "Thank you Sir."

"Have you learned anything?"

"I don't know, I am so confused Sir" she replied honestly.

"Confused because you liked being spanked?"

"Maybe, it hurt, but…" she stopped, not able to admit how she was really feeling.

"But you are hornier now than you were before I spanked your ass?" he said, completing her thought in a rather vulgar way. Oddly though, she liked the way he said it.

"Yes Sir," she replied, again honestly.

"Well, you honored your part of the bargain. Now you have a choice to make, either you can take your panties and go home, and we will go our separate ways.

Or, you can stand up, take off the rest of your clothes, kneel at my feet, and then beg me to teach you more about yourself."

The first part of his offer was not something she wanted to do, but the alternative was a daunting proposition. She understood what it would mean to strip, kneel, and beg him to school her in his dark world. She had no doubt that being with him required that she surrender to him, and though it was an exciting idea, she was still unsure if she could handle it. Her butt was aching, and she expected what he did was mild compared to what he would do if she fully submitted to him.

Still unsure whether to accept his offer, she asked, "Can we do a trial run?"

"That is what tonight is about silly girl. If you choose to continue, I will show you a sample of what to expect from me. When we are done we will both decide if we want it to go forward. Now stop dawdling and make your choice!"

Robyn felt foolish when he answered her, and now that she knew that he was only talking about tonight, it became an easy decision. She kicked off her shoes before using her arms to sit up and then stand beside the ottoman. She saw he was staring at her smiling, and she returned it with one of her own, as she slipped the spaghetti straps of her dress off her shoulders. Once her arms were free from the straps, she shimmied the dress down her body, trying to look sexy while she did. Once it was pooled on top of her bare feet, she kicked it aside and reached between her breasts to unclasp her bra, tossing it away next.

Before she could kneel, he said, "Stop! Link your fingers together behind your neck, arch your back, and slowly turn around until I tell you to stop."

"Yes Sir," Robyn replied, her voice dripping with lust. She was not the least bit ashamed to be showing off her naked body to George, in fact, she wanted him to see all of her.

As she began to spin around, she felt kind of foolish, but then he said, "You have a superb body girl, no doubt built for sex. The question is, what is your mind made for? Now close your eyes and continue to turn."

"Yes Sir," she answered breathlessly, as she closed her eyes and realized that she was a little dizzy. But not from the rotations, it was George that was making her head spin. This was so strange and deviant, but her body felt like a live wire, crackling with desire. She made a couple of revolutions more, not realizing that George stood up to face her as she turned.

When she was within his reach, he grabbed the sides of her head and planted his lips on hers, spearing his tongue into her mouth. It took her a moment for her to respond, but she quickly began twirling her tongue around his in a passionate wrestling match. Once they started, he moved one hand behind her head, and then used the other to pull her body against his, making sure she could feel the erection in his pants pressing against her bare belly.

After a long and ardent kiss, he pulled back and looked into her eyes. He could see how much it affected her, and when she whispered a thank you for it, he was very pleased. He was even more pleased that she still had her hands locked behind her neck, never attempting to embrace him during such a hot lip lock seemed like another sign that she was an inherently submissive girl.

In response, he said, "It is time to teach you a few more lessons girl."

CHAPTER 3: LEARNING THE ROPES

After saying that, he spun her around to face away from him and then he removed his tie. He grabbed her wrists and separated her hands before twisting them together again at the base of her back. He used the tie to secure her crossed wrists to each other, and she offered no resistance. George saw it as another good sign. Once her wrists were tied, he spun her back around and took the opportunity to squeeze her tits.

"OOOH! Thank you Sir!" she cooed, once again loving the feel of his hands on her flesh. And since it was her breasts this time, it felt truly incredible!

"You are a hot little slut, aren't you Robyn?" he asked.

A few hours ago, she would have considered that an insult, but given what was going on, how could she deny it? Sensing he expected a reply, she said, "Yes Sir! I am a hot little slut!"

"We are about to find out," he said, as he removed his belt and wrapped it around her throat.

Using the belt like a leash, he led her out of his study and up to his bedroom. As she tried to keep up with his brisk pace, she hoped that she would soon be screwing him. All she could think about was how badly she wanted it. And she didn't want soft and gentle love making either, she wanted him to take her hard and rough. Images from the videos she had watched were fueling her imagination, and being tossed around like a rag doll was what she was picturing in her mind.

When they reached his bedroom she was impressed with his huge four poster king size bed, and once they were next to it, she noticed the mirrored ceiling above it. He backed her up at the foot of it, right in the middle, and ordered her to sit. It was a high bed, so it was a bit challenging to sit down with her wrists tied behind her back, but she wiggled her way up onto the mattress, which left her feet dangling just above the floor.

He left her there and walked over to a cabinet, while saying, "A big part of what I like is bondage, tying up sexy women before playing with them. Are you up for that Robyn?"

She already liked the way her wrists were tied, so she answered, "Yes Sir."

"I figured as much, I do believe you will learn an awful lot about what really makes you tick tonight," he said, as he retrieved four leather cuffs and a few coils of rope from the cabinet before returning to the bed.

He sat beside Robyn and reached behind her back to untie her wrists. Then he got up and took each wrist, fastening the thick leather cuffs to each one. Next, he knelt down and put the cuffs on her ankles. After that, he stood up and tied the end of a coil of rope to the ring in her right wrist cuff, and did the same with another coil to the left one. He casually tossed the ropes onto the bed behind her, before moving to one side of the bed.

He said, "Lay on your back and stretch your arms out above your head."

Robyn was again functioning in a trance like state, as it felt more like a dream than reality. His voice was intoxicating, and whatever he said dictated her actions, not her own will. As she reclined backward and lifted her arms above her head, she felt like she was plunging into a dark pool of depravity. Her normal sensibilities were being overrun by her attraction to George, she just knew that he had a connection with her unlike any she ever experienced with anyone else.

Once Robyn was on her back, she felt her left arm pulled upward until it was stretched out and toward the side of the bed above her head. George tied the end of the rope to a ring bolt screwed into the side of the bedframe, one of the many attached along the edge of the bed. When that arm was done, he walked around the bed and tied off the other, admiring how Robyn was reacting. She had her eyes closed and she remained still, but he could see her breath quickening from the way her tits rapidly rose and fell against her chest.

He moved to the foot of the bed and took her right ankle, lifting it up and holding it, while he tied another coil of rope to the cuff. Then he threaded the loose end through another ringbolt mounted near the top of the footpost before tying it off, so that her leg was pulled outward and up a few feet above the mattress. After doing the same to her other ankle, she was left totally exposed and completely helpless. It was not really the ropes and cuffs that bound her, it was him, but now she was scared to open her eyes and look at him.

She felt his hand slide under her head and tilt it forward just before he slipped a firm pillow under her neck. When he removed his hand, Robyn knew she was facing down her body, and opening her eyes became an even more terrifying prospect. The trouble was, she liked the feeling of being bound like this, it felt dangerous and exhilarating. The way her sex had peeled open made it twitch just from the feeling of the air in the room caressing it. She was pretty sure that she had never been this horny before, and she liked the way it felt.

Then she heard him say, "Open your eyes girl!"

Robyn snapped her eyes open and saw he was sitting at the foot of the bed, right in front of her lewdly displayed pussy. Her view was right through her cleavage, and she could also see that her nipples were engorged and she could feel them also tingling. In all her life she never had to deal with so many sensations, all of which were emanating from her achingly hot sex. Her rump was still tender and sore, but at least it was not carrying any weight with her legs holding it up just above the mattress.

"Look at that cute trimmed bush, so you are a natural redhead," he commented.

"Yes Sir, I am," she replied, almost proudly.

"Are redheads as hot as they say they are?"

"I don't know Sir, but I am pretty hot for you right now Sir," she answered, trying hard to be both honest and earnest with him.

"I can see, your cunt is quite juicy looking. I bet you would love for me to shove my cock into it, wouldn't you?"

"Yes Sir!" Robyn cried out, having had enough of the foreplay, she wanted him inside her!

"Patience little slut, you will get my cock when you earn it. How often do you masturbate?" he asked, and her look of shock made him smile. Before she ventured an answer, he added, "Daily is my bet."

"Yes Sir, every day Sir," she said, feeling humiliated by admitting it, but even that stoked her arousal higher too.

"What kind of toys do you use?"

Though she wanted to scream, 'FUCK ME PLEASE,' she instead meekly said, "Some dildos and vibrators Sir."

"I see, so tell me, have you ever been with a man?" he asked.

"No Sir," she admitted, not sure if he would be scared away by a virgin.

"Well, in that case, it sounds like this pussy has seen a lot of action for a virgin. Have you ever experienced multiple orgasms during your self-gratification sessions?"

"Not really Sir, but I have masturbated more than once a day, sometimes three or four," she replied, wondering why it was so easy to admit her most private secrets to George. She still wanted him to ravage her, but he was making her bare her soul, and it felt good letting him know how hopelessly horny she was all the time.

"How many did you have between our first meeting and dinner?"

The look of shock and awe in her eyes was priceless, and her reply was simple, "Two Sir."

"Girl, you definitely need to learn some discipline, no wonder you want me to shag you so badly! But before we get to that, I want to find out how orgasmic you really are. Now, relax while I get some of *my* toys."

Robyn watched him return to the cabinet, while she tested her bonds, tugging on her wrist and ankle bindings. She realized how helpless she was, and though it was a little scary, something about George made her feel safe. Sure, she was bound in the lewdest way she could think of, but somehow she knew that he was about to release all the pent up desire that was building up inside her ever since he opened his front door earlier in the day.

George returned with a cardboard box, which he placed on the bed next to Robyn, but in her position she could not see what was in it. He took his seat between her widely splayed legs and reached into the box. He pulled out a gag with a bright red ball, and showed it to her. Her perusal of internet porn made her aware of gags just like this. Although being robbed of her voice was scary, she also knew that seeing gagged girls on the web was kind of sexy too. She was beginning to wonder why she never realized how much she was actually into these kinky things.

"I am going to gag you so that you do not embarrass yourself. Once I get you going, I am pretty sure you will think you can't handle it. The bondage and gag will ensure that you cannot stop me from pushing you to a level of sexual ecstasy that will be far more intense than anything you ever felt. Now be a good girl and open up your mouth," he said, as he leaned forward and moved the red ball toward her lips.

Robyn opened her mouth, as he instructed, but she was very nervous now, and not being able to speak would make her even more helpless. And, as he stated, she now expected that what was coming would overwhelm her, but deep down, she wanted to be pushed beyond her limits. Given that she had no idea what her limits were, she clung to the idea of 'sexual ecstasy.' She was hoping that he would satisfy her mounting desire to learn what that actually meant. Once he strapped it behind her neck, she could already feel her saliva leaking down over her chin.

Then he pulled a blindfold out of the box, and she shuddered at the prospect of being deprived of her sight too. But then he said, "What I am going to do will be about making you feel good, and the blindfold will make it easier to experience those feelings without distractions. Also, not knowing where or when a sensation will come from will add a level of anticipation that will enhance the overall effect," as he reached forward and covered her eyes with it.

The darkness that Robyn was plunged into was terrifying at first, but once it was on, she felt his hands rubbing her inner thighs. His touch was even more electrifying now that she could only feel what he was doing, and she started to understand what he meant. She also began to see that this was how he was seducing her, though not in any normal way, but definitely in a way that increased the sexual arousal building inside her.

"Now let's see how a virginal slut climaxes," he said.

Robyn felt something pressed against her sex just before she heard a click and the vibrator roared to life. Her whole body tensed up, and she moaned loudly into her gag, as her clitoris was inundated by the powerful vibrations and reacted by sending her into her first climax faster than she ever imagined possible. Even though she was tightly bound, she still had some mobility, and she began writhing her hips to escape the intensity of the orgasm that erupted from her crushed love bud. She felt his arms pressing against her thighs, as she struggled with all her might to escape the sensations that assailed her tiny little clit. But then he pulled it away, yet the orgasm raged on, and she kept on twitching uncontrollably.

"My bad," he said, "Try and relax while I make you a bit more secure."

She had no idea how to relax in that moment, her whole body was buzzing with sexual energy since that orgasm was the best she ever had! She could not believe how quickly it happened, or how strong it was, and she began to understand why he wanted her tied up for it. She wanted to curl up into a little ball, and she knew she would have thrashed about wildly if she had not been tied to the bed.

She felt him wrap straps around her upper thighs, and then she felt them pulled downward, further restricting her ability to move. Once her thighs were secured, Robyn tested her added bondage and realized she could no longer move her hips. She regretted writhing the way she did when that first orgasm hit her like a bolt of lightning, but he didn't seem to blame her. Now that he fixed the problem, she expected another assault was coming.

Instead, she felt his fingers exploring the folds of her sex, peeling apart her labia and caressing the moist entrance to her vagina. Then she felt him dip a finger into the opening of her sex, and she began moaning loudly. He was just gently stroking her sex, but it was already

41

stoking up another orgasm, and she welcomed the pleasure that was building up inside her again. Then she felt the finger retreat, and it disappointed her.

"You really have a perfect pussy slut, one that needs to get fucked hard and often," he said, and he smiled when she nodded her agreement. "But you are also undisciplined and I will have to address that shortcoming if you decide to become my trainee after tonight. Let's see how it goes now that you can't wiggle your way out of it."

This time she heard him turn on the vibrator, but instead of pressing it against her clit, he rubbed one of her nipples with it. A loud moan and another muscle tensing reaction followed, as he massaged one, and then the other nipple with the powerful vibrator. It was almost as intense as it felt on her clit, and she definitely felt her pussy lubricating while her nipples were being buzzed.

"That's a good slut, feel the how pleasure in your nipples is making your cunt quiver with desire. There are many ways to goad a horny slut like you into an orgasm, and if you choose to follow my lead, we will explore all of them."

Robyn felt like she was floating on a cloud, this was the most erotic moment of her life, despite the fact that she was trussed up and unable to contribute. She was under his control, and she did not have to worry about how she performed because she could not. It was a strangely liberating feeling, allowing him to do everything, while she just laid back and enjoyed it. She remembered how worried she was when she first sucked her boyfriend's cock, and every time they hooked up for that matter. With George, all she had to do was let him rock her world, and he was certainly doing that!

For a few moments she felt and heard nothing other than the sound of him getting something else from the box next to her. Then she felt a finger penetrate her sex again, and she moaned in appreciation, it was like her pussy was on the edge, and any sensation it felt was being incredibly amplified. But then it slipped out of her sex and slid down over her perineum, just before it started to prod her sphincter.

"Did you know the anus is also an erogenous zone?" he asked, as he pushed his finger through the tight muscle at the end of her rectum. She groaned this time, but as tight as it felt, the sensation of his finger inside her anus actually felt really good.

He began slowly prodding her anus with his index finger, noting how it was making her pussy wink at him, and caused her juices to seep from her gaping gash. Her initial groan was quickly displaced by moans of pleasure, and she began to believe what he just said. She could feel how the finger massaging her butt hole was also stimulating her pussy just above it, and it was a powerful surprise for the naïve girl. She had never even considered playing with her asshole, but thanks to George, she now wanted to explore another type of arousal.

Robyn was lost is a sea of strange and exotic sensations, all of them conspiring to elevate her arousal in ways she still did not believe possible. Even before he started toying with her, she wanted to feel him fuck her, and though she had not forgotten, just following his lead was incredibly exciting. As his finger loosened up her anal muscle, and she reveled in her new perverse sexuality, he took another item from the box.

When he withdrew his finger from her anus he was ready to insert the new toy, a small anal plug with a built in vibrator. Robyn groaned when the widest part of the plug stretched her anal muscle open, but once it seated inside her ass at the narrow end, she kind of purred. George just stared at her, and saw how she was flexing her sphincter against the rubber intruder.

For her edification, he said, "That is a butt plug, how do you like it?"

His answer was a moan of pure satisfaction, as Robyn liked how the plug felt nestled tightly inside her bottom. Maybe because it was pressing against the bottom of her pussy too, and by squeezing against it, it was making her sex feel even better. This unexpected lesson in some of the ways he could get her all hot and bothered was too much for her to fully process, and she had to abandon thinking very much, as she just focused on the many sensations assailing her body.

"I think you will like it more in a moment," he said, and then he turned it on, and poor little Robyn shuddered from the newest sensation.

It was totally unexpected, and the power of the vibrations from her rectum moved upward, making her pussy buzz almost as forcefully. All her muscles locked up and she knew she could not resist the orgasm that was about to hit her, and when it did, her scream was barely muffled by her gag. The pleasure exploded inside her like a super nova and even blindfolded, she saw starbursts, it was a feeling she would never be able to properly describe.

But George was not done, and as her anal orgasm sent her to stratospheric heights, he began slapping her sex with the palm of his hand. Not hard, but enough to create a wet smacking sound and make Robyn buck and shudder. Sure, it stung her sensitive sex, but it also propelled her orgasm to even greater heights. He could see that she was starting to have multiple orgasms, almost every slap against her bright pink sex instigating a new climax.

Robyn was in a place she could not believe, as wave after wave of pleasure coursed through her body. Sure, there was some pain every time the hand smacked her sex, but the orgasms that followed were like plunging into a vat of white hot ecstasy. It was so intense that she soon wanted it to stop, but then another climax would hit and she wanted more. It was like trying to tread water in a stormy sea, with the water trying to pull her down while she struggled to stay afloat.

George pussy slapped Robyn into a delirium, marveling at how perversely orgasmic this girl was, and especially how she got there. When he began slapping her twat, he just intended to amplify the orgasm her vibrating butt plug prompted. The multiple orgasms she had from his slaps was wholly unexpected, but it was at that moment that he decided that she might very well be the one he sought. He stopped slapping her and then licked her tart pussy juice from the palm of his hand, as he watched her twitching in the aftermath of her explosive sexual outburst.

She seemed like she was still awake, as she kept turning her head on the pillow, and he figured if he released her she would sleep for a while. Then he remembered her anal plug was still buzzing inside her rectum and he decided to give her the knockout blow. He picked up the vibrator, turned it on high, and jammed it right up against her clit.

"MMMMMMMRRRRRRGGGGGGG!" Robyn growled like an animal, as her body went rigid once again. Her spanked pussy had increased sensitivity, and when the buzzing ball pressed against it, she was launched into another total body orgasm. She thrashed against her bindings, as the energy of the orgasm demanded physical release. The bed creaked from her gyrations, but her bonds held firm, as George vibrated her into mental and emotional oblivion!

When she finally went limp, apart from a few involuntary twitches, George finally stopped both vibrators and released her from the bondage. He gently slid her limp body to the head of the bed and gently tucked a pillow under her head. Then he covered her with a sheet, and once she was tucked in, he walked downstairs.

He went to his workshop and began tinkering with a few things he designed now that he found the right candidate. Robyn was definitely something special, in under an hour he wiped her out with hardly any effort. It told him two things, the first was that she was woefully inexperienced. And the other, she was a sexual firecracker, and one that responded well to a firm hand.

He was still shocked how she kept climaxing when he spanked her pussy, it was incredible!

He was fairly certain that she would want more, and she still owed him for all he did for her so far. He decided that he would test her commitment by denying her the fuck she wanted and making her earn it. He already came up with a plan, and all he had to do was make a few adjustments to the things he had designed for his first real trainee. It was looking more and more likely that the sleeping teen in his bed would eventually become the trainee he sought.

CHAPTER 4: MAKING A CHOICE

When Robyn woke up, nearly ten hours after she passed out, she was a little panicked. She was naked and in a strange bed with her memory of the prior night just starting to come back to her. When her recall clarified and she had a clearer picture of what actually happened, she reached down between her legs and groaned when she found her pussy was still tender and sore. She looked around the room, remembering how she was brought here on a leash.

Then Robyn got worried, wondering if he fucked her after she blacked out, she thought her pussy felt tender enough for that to be possible. She doubted he would do that, but then again, he did a lot of things that were pretty far off the beaten path. She wondered why she could not think about it for what it was, he was a kinky dominant man that wanted a submissive plaything. Robyn was still in a post erotic euphoria, and the idea of submitting to George was now very tempting.

She didn't see her clothes anywhere, and she had to go to the bathroom. Since no one was around and her bladder was insistent, she bolted into the ensuite bathroom in the buff, shutting the door behind her. She groaned all through her pee, even that hole was sore after what he did to her. Her butt felt strange too, normally she only noticed it when she had to poop, but this morning it also felt tender. After she finished her toilet, she went to the sink and looked at her reflection.

She grimaced because she was a hot mess, so she ran the water and grabbed a hand towel, taking some time to wash her face. Robyn was amazed the flower clip was still attached to her hair, and grateful that she could gather her disheveled mane and clip it into some semblance of order. Then she looked at her sex, it was still swollen and bright pink. A quick twist to look at her rump revealed no signs of the spanking, and given how bad it hurt, she remembered his comment about not damaging her.

Once Robyn thought she looked somewhat respectable, she opened the door and went back into the bedroom. And there he was, sitting on chair next to a small table on the far side of the room. There was a coffee service on the table and she could smell the aroma of a freshly brewed pot wafting through the room. She thought that she could really use a cup of coffee, but seeing him sitting there smiling at her compelled her to wait for him to say something first.

"You look beautiful like that Robyn," he said, and she suddenly realized she was still totally naked. She instinctually moved one arm over her breasts and the other hand to cover her pubic mound, but he was having none of it, and snapped, "Put your arms behind your back girl!"

Robyn immediately obeyed, as his voice, especially in this tone, compelled her to do what he demanded. She stared at him in fear and awe, he had some strange power that made her want to obey him. He was the only person she ever met that made her feel so weak and helpless, but she was starting to understand that her sassy nature was a masquerade. It worked on most people, but George saw right through it and she could not resist the power that she felt emanating from him.

"You made quite a spectacle of yourself last night Robyn. What do you have to say about it?" he asked.

"Yes Sir, thank you Sir, it was…eye opening," Robyn answered, still trying to be coy.

"It certainly was from my perspective too, but you passed out before you could show me your appreciation for what I did for you. Now get down on your hands and knees and crawl over here to me," he said, as he pointed to the floor between his legs.

"Yes Sir!" Robyn chirped, as she dropped to her knees and crawled over to George.

George watched the sexy teen crawling to him, liking the way she slinked her way to him with her tits swaying nicely beneath her body. When she reached him he said, "Kneel and face me you hot little slut."

Robyn would have cringed and lashed out at anyone else calling her a slut, but somehow, when he said it, she liked it. He certainly made her feel like one, just being in his presence made her feel like a cheap whore. As she assumed the position he dictated, Robyn's strange compulsion to obey him was irresistible. When she stared into his eyes, it was like they looked into her soul, and he knew what made her tick. It was a dynamic that made her feel more alive than ever.

"Look at you, naked and kneeling at my feet. How does it feel Robyn?" he asked her.

"It feels good Sir," she answered, driven by a new need that, until yesterday, had been dormant inside her.

"What did you learn from our little encounter last night?" he asked, wanting her to reveal her newfound desires to him.

"I learned that you understand me in ways that even I did not. I also discovered that when I am with you, I feel more alive than ever, and sexier than I thought I could feel."

"That is a good place to start Robyn. But before we go any farther, you need to know the rules that will define a relationship with me. Do you want to hear the rules slut?"

"Yes Sir," she meekly replied, as she realized that she was all hot and bothered again.

"Good, now listen carefully. First and foremost, if you ultimately choose to be with me that will be the last choice you will make. Once you swear allegiance to me, I will be your will, all you do will be under my direction. Disobedience or resistance will not be tolerated, and any infractions will result in a punishment. Is that clear?"

"Yes Sir."

"The next part is even harder. Those gentle spankings I gave you last night, on your ass and your cunt, were minor compared to what I will do to you if you decide to become mine. I am seeking a girl that can handle being treated roughly and can also tolerate humiliation as the norm. Is that clear *slut?*" he asked, emphasizing the demeaning term at the end.

"Yes Sir," Robyn replied, feeling both frightened and elated.

Even though he was promising more, and worse, pain, not to mention the demeaning verbal abuse, she could not deny that the proposition was bizarrely exciting. She understood the concept of submission, but these rules clarified what that actually meant. And even though he required her absolute submission, she was still captivated by him and eager to learn what he could teach her about these potent new feelings he provoked from her.

"Now, and this is the hardest part, I am part of a community of like-minded people. That means that you will join it too. That will require you to submit to whoever I tell you to. You will be mine, but I will share you with others. Can the slut handle that?"

Robyn was dumbstruck by his last comment, and it was a frightening prospect, at first. But as she stared at him, imagining being given to someone else by him sounded kind of sexy. But she was still a girl that had yet to copulate with anyone, and he was telling her that if she followed him that she would have to sexually service others. The fact that he asked if she could handle it gave her pause, but she was so drawn to him that her desire continued to prevail.

"Yes Sir, I think so," she said, trying to convey that she had no way to know for sure that she could handle it.

"Does that condition worry the slut?"

"Yes Sir."

"Let me ask you this, if you remember how you were feeling last night, do you think you would have flinched if I brought another man in to play with you too?"

Robyn flashed back to the night before, remembering how hot and horny she felt. She doubted that if another man joined in that she would have cared in the least. He was devilishly good at making her see things from a different perspective. In that light, she answered, "No Sir, I would not have cared."

"I appreciate your honesty Robyn, and that is the lynch pin of a relationship like the one I am proposing. I will give you a promise; I will not share you with anyone until I am sure you are trained and ready for it. And that is what you will agree to, becoming my trainee. But you must also accept that you know nothing, so I can teach you how to embrace your submissive role. You have it buried inside you and I can release it, and then I will unleash it"

His promise made it easier to digest the idea of being shared. His voice continued to magnify her attraction to him, and it compelled Robyn to say, "Yes Sir! I can handle it."

"Then tell me slut, do you want to become my slave?" he asked.

When he said the word 'slave,' Robyn felt a tremor of lust well up inside her. That word sounded so much more intense than submissive! She had been avoiding thinking about it that way, but this moment demanded that she be honest with herself. He had opened a door to a new reality, one she never imagined, but it was clearly part of her and it was taking over all her sensibilities. She had no idea why she suddenly wanted to surrender all her freedom and agree to follow George blindly, but the compulsion to be under his control was too hard to resist.

Looking up into his eyes, she said, "Yes Sir, please train me to become your slave."

"Are you sure slut?"

"Yes Sir, I want to serve you," she said in a very kittenish tone of voice.

"Then I accept you into my service. I will draw up a full set of rules for you and you will memorize and abide by them. But now we must address your failure from last night. Do you know what you failed to do?"

It was painfully obvious, especially in this proximity to his crotch. She could see that he was hard inside his pants and she wanted to jump his bones so badly that it took all her self-control to remain kneeling humbly at his feet. Robyn wanted to answer, 'I never got to fuck you Sir,' but somehow that felt inappropriate given her new status.

So, she said, "I did not sexually service you Sir."

"She is learning, but I am sure you were thinking more specifically, so say it."

"We never got to…fuck Sir," she stammered, feeling the blush infuse her cheeks.

"Honesty is always best, remember that slut."

"Yes Sir," she replied, even though he was starting to confuse her again.

"Normally, I would shag your cunt silly right now, but given your inexperience on every level I think some training would be better for you first. Not only do you have no idea what this lifestyle entails, but you are still basically a virgin. When I take you I want to know, without a doubt, that you are fully committed to this. Right now, you are on a sexual high, you need time to fully accept the role you just chose. So, for now, your mouth will please me, and when I decide you are ready, I will take you completely. Is that clear?"

"Yes Sir," Robyn answered dejectedly, almost in tears.

"Is the slave sad?"

"Yes Sir, I want you so badly," she confessed, and then the tears did come.

"Here is another lesson for you, as my slave, you must learn to subvert your desires in favor of mine. This will test your true resolve to become what I want. You must also learn *self-discipline,* not just the restraints I will place on you. I will give you one last chance to back out, if all you want is a cheap fuck, then you aren't meant for me."

That comment was like a punch to her gut, as Robyn faced the fact that she had always been selfish, always pursuing her own desires regardless of the situation. This was going to be a huge leap in the opposite direction, and she was now finding out how hard it would be. He did not deny that he wanted her, but he was clear that he thought that she was not ready yet. If she really wanted him to teach her how to be a slave, she had to accept that he knew what his desires were and that meant they had to be hers too.

"I accept your decision Sir. I am not yet ready to be...fucked by you. Please train me to be worthy enough to feel your cock inside my...cunt."

"You are an interesting creature Robyn; I have never encountered a slut quite like you."

"Thank you Sir," she replied, not sure if he was actually complimenting her.

"Now you may remove my cock from my pants and suck it. That will show me how grateful you are to become my slave."

"Yes Sir, thank you Sir," she answered, suddenly feeling much better. She had been dying to feel his cock for weeks, and even if her sex was denied it, at least her hands and mouth would be able to satisfy both of their desires.

Robyn started to unzip him, but he slapped her hands and pointed at the belt of his pants. She immediately moved her hands up and unclasped his belt and khakis, feeling he had a point about her inexperience. She even had to learn how to get his erection out of his slacks, a thought that forced her to accept her naïveté. She had always blustered her way through her life, not really knowing what she should do, chiefly acting on her feelings. And so far, it just made things more difficult, and letting him take over that responsibility was becoming a more attractive option.

Once she finally lowered his zipper, he lifted his butt off the chair and she took the cue, pulling his pants down to his ankles. Once they were halfway down, he lowered his butt and lifted his feet off the floor. She knew that he expected her to remove them completely, which she gladly did. She had just caught a glimpse of his cock, while pulling his pants down his thighs, and it was gorgeous. She slid the pants to the side and he put his feet back down, then he parted his legs.

"No hands, just your mouth," he said. Although that was another desire of hers quashed, at least her mouth would get to experience the firm staff in front of her face.

Robyn did not feel the way she did now when she was sucking her boyfriend's cock at school, but then again, when he went down on her it wasn't that great either. But now she really wanted to suck George's cock, partly in appreciation for what he did for her the night before, but also because she wanted to please him. It was such a change of attitude that it was hard to believe that she was actually feeling this way.

Robyn was about to place her hands on his thighs, but something inside her stopped her, and she folded them behind her back instead. He smiled at her when she did that, and she took it as a sign that what she just did pleased him. She looked at his staff and licked her lips before leaning forward, happy when he bent it down so that it was aimed right at her mouth. She parted her lips and slid it between them, licking it with her tongue along the underside of his dick, as it entered her warm, moist mouth. She began to bob up and down, but she was only able to get about half of it into her mouth before she started to gag and pulled back.

After she was passionately sucking his cock, he said, "You can add cock sucking to your list of insufficiencies, but your enthusiasm is noted."

Robyn felt a mix of emotions, his half-hearted compliment was nice, but once again he was pointing out how unprepared she was for all this. He was making her feel both small and special, and she was trying to accept that it was only because of her inexperience. But she still had doubts that she would ever meet his expectations, unaware that was exactly what he wanted. Her own naiveté was impeding her ability to recognize how he was playing with her mind, as she had yet to realize that the mental aspect of this life was what gave it such a potent influence over her.

George was actually enjoying his blow job more than he thought he would. Looking down at her back and how she mentally bound her arms behind it after he told her not to use them was interesting. It was another insight into her psyche, and it showed him that she really was paying attention and only doing what he specifically told her. Not that he would ever let her know, he had to make sure he was never predictable, since that would give her an edge no real slave of his could be allowed to have.

As much as he enjoyed her tender lips wrapped around his staff, George also wanted to get her training started, not that this was not part of it. But he had formulated an interesting plan for Robyn to learn what absolute submission was all about, and thinking about that helped him to achieve an orgasm. He gripped the sides of her head when he knew it was inevitable, and held it deep inside her mouth when it began to spew his spend into her throat.

When he gripped her head, Robyn knew what was coming, literally. She heard him order her to swallow it all, so once he had a firm grip on her skull, she clamped her lips as tightly as she could. His shaft felt amazing throbbing inside her mouth, especially since her pussy was twitching with desire at the same time. It felt wonderful and awful at the same time, as she really wanted him inside her sex! But, as she struggled to swallow his ample load, she reminded herself that she was pleasing him, and now that mattered more to her than her own gratification.

"Well little slave, once you swallow it all we can get your training started. Are you ready for a crash course in the art of slavery?"

Robyn moaned her affirmation, almost having an orgasm from the prospect of being trained by this man. He had captured her mind, body, and likely, her soul already. She could feel her own dark side taking control of her psyche. Her past actions had helped put her in this position, as she always gravitated to the rougher course, and this time she chose the hardest path possible. Though she had yet to realize how difficult it would become.

CHAPTER 5: LESSONS LEARNED

"That's enough slave, back off and face me," he said, and Robyn did what he ordered.

But before he could say anything else, she said, "Thank you Sir, your cock and your sperm were delicious."

"Well, you seem to have one important skill down pat. Sucking up to me is a good way to stay in my good graces. Now get back into the bathroom and take a shower, you smell like a cheap whore. And don't even think about playing with yourself while in there, those days are over. You will receive pleasure when I think you earned it, and right now, you have yet to earn a thing!"

"Yes Sir," she answered, as she got up and went to walk into the bathroom.

"Who said you could stand and walk?"

She stopped, frozen in confusion, and she said, "No one Sir."

"Then get back down on your hands and knees and crawl into the shower. In fact, stay on your hands and knees while you shower, and when you are done, don't bother drying off, just crawl down to the kitchen where I will be waiting for you," he said sternly.

Robyn dropped to the floor again, and crawled into the bathroom, wondering how pissed off he was. He certainly sounded angry with her. It was strange showering on her hands and knees, she did have to just kneel to use her hands to wash, and she hoped that what she was doing would be acceptable to him. Though she was alone, she had the sense that he would know if she deviated from his instructions.

When she was done, she made sure her hair was soaking wet, and she used her hands to pull it back behind her head so it was somewhat neat. As it dried naturally, it would blossom into a mass of curls that hung down around her shoulders, so what she did was just a temporary fix. She felt a chill in the air when she crawled out of the bathroom, but overall, her endless arousal kept her warm enough. Even the fact that he was making her crawl around naked like a dog did not sway her desire to obey, she had already accepted that kinky games like this made her hot.

The journey to the kitchen was a little rough on Robyn's knees, there were rugs and hard wood floors to navigate, not to mention the stairs! She opted to back her way down, again unsure if that was the way he wanted, but she was still crawling as ordered. When she arrived in the kitchen she could smell bacon and eggs cooking, and more coffee! But she simply stopped just inside the room and waited for his next instruction, liking how nice it was not having to think about what she should do next.

"You may take a seat at the table; breakfast is almost ready. Would you like some coffee?"

"Yes Sir, thank you Sir. Coffee would be wonderful," she answered, as she crawled up onto the seat he pointed to.

He put a plate of scrambled eggs, bacon, and wheat toast in front of her. Then he poured her a cup of coffee, before filling his cup and finally returning with his plate and sitting across from her at the table. She noticed that he had a fork and knife, but she did not. She was so hungry, but she dared not touch her food or drink, she expected that he would tell her when and how to eat. It was all so strange and confusing, but she had committed to following his lead, and it obviously meant in every way.

With his eyes fixed on Robyn's, he took a sip of his coffee. She remained still and quiet, and then he put the cup down and said, "You are learning girl, now place your palms on the table beside your plate." Once she did what he told her, he said, "You may eat now."

Robyn knew what he expected from her, and she kind of liked how subtle he was about it. There was no doubt that her hands were unavailable for use, he told her to put them on the table and nothing else. She was not going to make the mistake she made in the bedroom, this time she would only do what he instructed. So, to eat her food, she bent down and began using her mouth to eat off the plate, just like an animal.

Once she started, he said, "That's a good slut. Clean your plate and you will be allowed to drink your coffee, and don't dawdle, we have work to do."

Robyn paused just long enough to say, "Yes Sir, thank you Sir." And as she ate her meal, those words ran through her mind. She had spoken them quite often already, but every time she did, it felt more and more natural. Even eating like a dog from her plate, though it was humiliating, still felt right because he wanted her to do it. He told her that he would humiliate her, and she started to wonder how far he would take it. She stopped that line of thought quickly, not wanting to contemplate what kind of degrading acts he might demand that she do for him.

George observed his potential trainee, and since he had committed to this course, that was what she was for now. Robyn managed to eat the bacon and eggs without much trouble, but the toast gave her some issues. She kept her head bowed over her plate the whole time, even as she fought to capture the toast that kept sliding around her plate. But she managed to eat it all, and what really impressed him was how she licked the whole plate clean before she stopped. And once she did finish, she remained facing down at her plate.

After waiting for a little while after she finished, he said, "You may sit up and drink your coffee, and you may use your hands again."

She lifted her head, looked into his eyes, while trying to ignore the food scraps stuck to her face. Once their eyes met, she said, "Thank you Sir, breakfast was delicious."

"Don't get used to it, you will learn to prepare my meals as part of your duties. So, tell me slave, are you beginning to understand the extent of what I require from you?"

"Yes Sir," she answered.

"And do you like it?"

"Very much Sir."

"I'm glad that my impression of you was so accurate, now you may wipe the crumbs off your face, and clean it up after you do."

"Yes Sir," she replied, as she bent over her plate and wiped her face off with her hand. Then, just like after she finished eating, she bent all the way down and licked those crumbs off the dish too.

George noticed that when she began licking up the facial crumbs, she put her hands back where they were beside the plate while she was eating. She was almost too good to be true, but he was just getting started and had much harsher tests planned for her already. Once the plate was clean again, she sat back up and looked at him like a puppy who just bonded with her owner, not that she was that much different than an animal in training.

"Go ahead, have some coffee now," George said.

"Yes Sir, thank you Sir," she replied, as she reached out to the spoon in the sugar bowl.

It was the mistake he expected, and he said, "Wait! Did you have permission to add sugar?"

Robyn froze again, caught by a habit of adding cream and sugar to her coffee. She had not even thought about it, but now she did, and she simply replied, "No Sir, but I always add cream and sugar and I forgot to ask."

"That's too bad, because today you will drink it black."

"Yes Sir," she replied, as she reached for the cup. It was a big mug actually, and she hated black coffee. But arguing about it seemed futile, so she drank it. It was nasty, hot, and bitter, it was not a pleasant experience at all. She could not hide her distaste for it, but he just smiled and watched her suffer through it, all the way down to the bottom of the mug. When she put the empty mug down, it was only after she tipped it upside down and licked every drop out of the cup.

"Was it that bad?" he asked.

"Yes Sir," she admitted, and now she wanted something to rinse it down with, but she dared not ask after her latest infraction.

As if he knew what she was thinking, he asked, "Would you like some orange juice to wash the bitterness away?"

"Yes Sir, if that is OK with you Sir," she answered.

He placed two wooden spring clothespins on her empty plate, and then said, "Attach these to your nipples and I will allow you to have some juice."

Robyn looked at them, and then up at him, and he only smiled at her. Though putting clothespins on her nipples was the last thing she wanted to do, she knew this was not about juice, it was about obedience. She reached forward and picked them up, squeezing them open to see how strong the springs were, glad that they did not feel too stiff. With the pins in hand, she looked down at her nipples. She saw how they were already engorged, stiff little nubbins that the clips would easily grip. They would also hurt like hell, of that she was sure, and she was about to prove it.

It felt like she was moving in slow motion, as the opened jaws of the pin surrounded her hard nipple. When she released it, she let out a small squeal, and shuddered, making it bounce up and down. She wanted to beg him to let her take it off, it felt worse than she thought, but she did not. She did put the other one on, and the combined effect left her whimpering kind of cutely.

"I know they hurt, but you are tough enough to handle it. Now stand up and go to the fridge and get out the bottle of juice. You will find glasses in the upper cabinet to the left of the fridge, get two, fill them, and bring them back to the table."

"Yes Sir," she replied, but then she stood up and gasped when she looked down at the seat.

"Made a mess did you?"

"Yes Sir, I am so sorry Sir!" she was mortified by the size of the puddle she left on the wooden seat, and she could also feel it trickling down her thighs now.

"Turn around," he said, and she did, revealing that the backs of her thighs were covered in girl juice. Once she did, he said, "Grab the towel on the counter and dry your thighs you messy little slut."

"Yes Sir, thank you Sir!" she replied and gladly used the towel to dry off her thighs.

Before she finished, he also said, "When they are dry you will lick up the mess you left on the chair."

She was almost done, but she stopped drying her legs, looked at him, and said, "Sir?"

"You heard me. Don't tell me you never tasted your cunt when you played with yourself in your bedroom," he said, sounding very annoyed.

"No Sir, I mean Yes Sir, I mean my nipples hurt Sir!" she exclaimed, as suddenly it all became too much and she almost freaked out.

As upset as Robyn became, George was more than pleased. He was beginning to wonder how hard he had to push to put her over the edge mentally. Apparently the right mixture of pain and humiliation did the trick, and he played his part to the hilt. He stood up abruptly, which sent his chair skidding backward. It got the reaction he wanted, as he could see the fear on her face. He walked over to her, staring at her angrily. He grabbed her throat and pushed her back until she hit a wall. Even though her initial reaction was to resist, once she was pinned against the wall her arms fell to her sides and she just stared at him with tears in her eyes.

He looked at her and said, "I told you this would not be easy. Are you going to be good, or am I going have to change my plans and punish you instead?"

"I'll be good," she whispered, his grip too tight to allow her to speak any louder. He was not choking her, but the way he held her did impede her breathing a little.

He let go of her neck and then flicked the clips on her nipples, making Robyn squeal and shudder. Then he said, "Then get on your knees, lick that seat clean, and then get me my damn juice! I will watch and tell you when you are done, now do it!"

"Yes Sir! Thank you Sir," Robyn replied loudly, his little show of strength just added to the grip he was establishing on her mind. As she dropped to the floor and began to crawl to her chair, he reached down and swatted her rump for good measure. When she thanked him for it, he smiled, and leaned against the wall to watch her lap up her own cunt juice. This girl was going to be a joy to train!

Robyn's nipples were screaming for release, but she dutifully lapped up her own sexual discharge, and was surprised that it was kind of exciting and not as gross as she imagined. The taste was kind of sweet and tart, and

67

though she had tentatively tasted her sex juices before, it was just a little, not the flood she was licking up now. Whatever was happening to her was not just mental or emotional, her pussy had never leaked like it just did in all her life. He was definitely having a physical impact on her, changing the way her body reacted to arousal.

"That's enough, time to fetch our juice slut," George said, giving her a small prod on her butt with his foot.

Robyn got up, and said, "Thank you Sir," then went to perform her original task, just like she had intended to before her sloppy cunt upset his orderly plan.

George returned to his seat, and when she came back and handed him his glass, he said, "Put the other glass down and sit on the chair, but grab that towel first and sit on it."

Though it was a practical request, it still added to the shame she felt. Not only was she a slut, she was an extremely messy one too! But, as she berated herself for leaking like a sieve, his voice cut through her befuddled mind again.

"Do not think I am displeased by your sloppy cunt. It is just your hidden desires bubbling to the surface to show you how much you need my guidance. Now drink your juice and maybe I will allow you to remove the clothespins."

"Yes Sir, thank you Sir," she said automatically, as it was already becoming a rote reply.

She downed the glass rather quickly, likely more eager to get the clamps off her teats rather than her simple enjoyment of the beverage. Once the glass was empty, licked clean of every drop, she put it back on the table and looked at him. He was smiling at her, and that made her feel better, but she was still oblivious as to what he planned next. She asked herself if that would always be the case, hoping that she could just find one thing that she could expect. The only answer she had was to expect the unexpected, and she had no idea how to do that!

"I am sure you are confused, and that is fine. Have you noticed that the pain in your nipples isn't as bad as it was at first?" he asked, directing her attention back to her pegged nubbins.

"Yes Sir, they still hurt, but not as much," Robyn replied, as she stared at her poor tit buds.

"In a minute I will allow you to remove them, but I warn you that it will make them hurt even more when you do. In order to ease that pain, you will hold up your tits and suck on your nipples once they are removed. Are those instructions clear slave?"

Robyn stared at him with another look of disbelief, appreciating the warning, but not so thrilled by the remedy he demanded. But, given what had already transpired, she had no desire to question his command, and she replied, "Yes Sir."

"Then you may remove the clips, use both hands and take them off at the same time," he said, really enjoying how he was toying with her mind and body.

Bracing herself, Robyn gripped the ends of the pins, closed her eyes, and squeezed them open simultaneously. The pain flared up almost immediately, as the blood rushed back into her nipples. But rather than screaming, she merely groaned in pain. Then she remembered the other part, so she dropped the pins onto the table and grabbed her aching tits. Then she bent over, and as her hands lifted her mounds, her lips wrapped around her right nipple. It stung at first, but once she licked and suckled it, the pain retreated. Once the first nipple felt better, she moved to the other, and sucked on it too.

"That is enough girl, now look at me," he said.

Robyn released her nipple from her mouth, and looked at him, but her hands remained on her tits. She kind of liked sucking on her nipples, and groping her tits too, thinking how she really was becoming a kinky little slut. Though she liked those videos with young girls being roughly screwed by older men, the kind of things he was making her do was much kinkier. Though she never fantasized about things like this, experiencing them was shockingly exhilarating!

"I hope this morning has been as illuminating to you as it has been for me. Maybe you now understand why you saw my previous guests disappear after our initial encounters. You have to be wired for this to appreciate it, and most women are not. But you, Robyn, definitely have an innate submissiveness built into your psyche. There is no way you would respond to me the way you have if you were not inherently submissive. Am I wrong?"

"I don't know Sir, but I think so. I have no idea why I am feeling like this, I never felt this way before, and I think that it may be true. But I don't think anyone else could make me feel this way, I only feel submissive because of you Sir."

"I am the catalyst, yes, but I just allowed the real you to come out of hiding. Are you ready to fully explore your new feelings slave?"

"Yes Sir, thank you Sir," she said, as she began to embrace the new feelings driving her.

CHAPTER 6: A SHORT DETOUR

"You will clean the dishes and kitchen now, and when you are done, come and find me in my study," he said. Then he got up and left her alone.

Robyn sat there for a few moments before she let go of her breasts and stood up to collect the dishes. It did not even occur to her that she was stark naked, as she carried the plates to the sink. She saw he had a dishwasher, but he told her to clean the kitchen, so she washed the plates, cups and his silverware by hand. She did notice how her nipples were still stinging, but for some odd reason, that feeling seemed to be prompting her sex to feel all swampy again.

She was still surprised by how incredibly horny she was, and Robyn wondered if she would always feel like this with him. Though he was not in the room with her, his presence loomed large in her mind, and that was triggering her physical reactions. Usually, in her past life, which was just yesterday, after a good orgasm her hunger was satisfied for at least a day. But since last night, after she had so many orgasms that she lost count, she was even hornier after she woke up in his bed. It was both disturbing and exciting, and she was beginning to think that was how it would always be if she really became his slave.

She finished her chores and she started to walk to the study. But she stopped after a few steps, dropped to her knees, and began crawling there instead. Something about crawling through his home in the buff felt erotic too, even though it was just a different way to move. It was not what she was doing, it was the meaning it conveyed to her, she was crawling for his pleasure. And for a girl who always put her needs and desires first, it was a colossal shift in her demeanor.

When she arrived in the study, Robyn saw him sitting in the chair where he was when she first stripped for him. She crawled over to the side of the seat, and when he pointed to the floor in front of him, she moved to kneel before him. Once she settled into position, Robyn realized how good it felt to just kneel at his feet, something she would have never even considered just yesterday.

"Is my kitchen clean?" he asked.

"Yes Sir."

"Good, now we must discuss how to proceed. Living here full time would expedite your training, but since you live across the street, you will spend nights there for the time being. Most of your day will be spent here, but you will go home to sleep," and as he spoke, he saw how that news was not what she wanted to hear. That was good, she needed to sublimate her desires anyway.

"But before we get started today, you need to go home and do a few things for me. In order to make it easier for me to monitor you, I have something for you," he said. Then held up something that looked like a hearing aid, but with an odd looking curved piece coming out of the bottom of it. "This is an earbud on an encrypted channel, so that you can hear my orders while at your house. It also has a camera, right here," pointing at the curved protuberance, "and with that, I will see what you see."

"Now use this," he said, as he held up an elastic band, and he added, "gather your hair behind your head and use it to keep your hair off your face."

As Robyn reached up and took it, she said, "Yes Sir."

She put the band between her lips, as she always did before gathering her hair into a tail. Once she had pulled it back, one hand kept it together, while the other grabbed the band and worked it over the clumped end of her mane. Once she had the band in place she lowered her hands and watched him fit the device into her ear, it felt a little strange, but not uncomfortable in the least. He picked up his phone and began tapping the screen, and then he smiled.

"Perfect, can you hear me in your earbud slave?"

"Yes Sir," she answered, but it was weird hearing the echo of two voices, both live and from the earbud.

George turned the phone so she could see the screen and she saw that she was staring at him and the phone. He said, "I will see and hear what you do slave, so I will be with you every step of this little errand you are about to run for me. Do you have a couple of travel bags?"

"Yes Sir, I have a gym bag and a backpack."

"That will do. You should know that I saw your parents' servants drive away a little while ago, how much do you interact with them?"

"Very little Sir, it is kind of like we share the same house, but live totally separate lives."

"That will make things easier, but for you to transition to living here, we will concoct a scenario where they think you have gone elsewhere. For today though, your mission is simple. You will walk to your house, go to your room, and do exactly what I instruct when you arrive. Can you handle that?"

"Yes Sir, do I have to do it naked?" she asked, since he did not tell her that she could dress. She did not realize how dependent on him she was becoming, but when he laughed at her comment, she kind of felt good that she had amused him in some way.

"Your clothes are over there," he said, pointing to a chair in the corner. "You may crawl over and put them back on now, and once you do, you may walk again," he said, thinking that she was surprising him almost as much as he was bewildering her.

"Yes Sir, thank you Sir," she replied, liking the sound of that statement more every time.

Robyn crawled to the chair, got up onto her knees, and picked up the bra. She put it on, and then picked up the dress, which she put on by pulling it down over her head. Once it was somewhat situated on her body, she sat down and slid the panties up her legs, lifting her butt just enough to get them over her rump. She slipped on her pumps, and then finally stood up and walked back to stand before George. As she walked, she smoothed out the dress and made sure it was properly situated on her body.

"You still look sexy in that dress, not as alluring as in the nude, but you can't be naked in public. Are you ready for your little trip?"

"Yes Sir, thank you very much Sir," she said, adding a superlative to it because of his positive compliment.

"Then it is time to go, follow me," he said, as he led her to the front door.

They walked to the door and he opened it and Robyn saw it was bright and sunny outside. But as pretty as it looked, she saw it in a different way now, as she had changed since she entered this house last night. She had entered his dark world, but now she had to go back out into the real one and it strangely scared her. Not enough to deter her from the task at hand, but enough that she wanted to get it over with and get back here as quickly as she could.

Her woolgathering at the door prompted George to say, "What are you waiting for slave? Get going!"

"Yes Sir, sorry Sir," Robyn replied, and then she started walking. Even the feeling of the sun on her body felt odd, so much about her was changing that it was hard to believe. He said nothing to her for the whole jaunt across the road and into her house, though she hoped he would not remain quiet for long. She was realizing how much she enjoyed hearing him speak to her, even when he was mean to her.

It was not until she reached her bedroom that he choose to speak, and he said, "What a nice room for a little girl."

She looked around after he said it, and she had to agree. It was painted in a pastel green with posters of pop stars and frilly curtains, and again she saw it in a new light. This was a child's room and she no longer felt like one, she did not consider herself a woman yet, but she hoped that George would show her how to become one. Not the kind she used to want to be, but the kind that allowed her man to take the lead. She used to scoff at that idea of the fifties-style housewife, but all she wanted now was to let him make all the decisions.

"Now collect all your sex toys and lay them on the bed so I can see them," he said.

Robyn kind of expected that, and she got down on her hands and knees and pulled the bag out from under her bed, where she kept them. She got up, opened it, and the spilled the contents onto the bed. Knowing he could see what she was seeing, she scanned the pile, waiting for her next instruction.

"My, my, that is quite a collection little girl, now pack it all up, you will bring it all back with you," he said, and then he watched her refill the bag. "Now let's look at your wardrobe, just the sexiest clothes and lingerie."

Robyn expected this too, and went to her closet, pulling out the most revealing dresses that were in it. She held each one up, and he would say yes or no, and the yes dresses would move to his house. Once they went through her dresses, she showed him her sexiest shorts, and he told her to bring them all. The same went for her sexy lingerie, and once she was done, the only clothes that would remain were her 'little girl' garments.

"Now pack up the clothes you are bringing back."

"Yes Sir," she said happily, hoping she would be back in his house soon.

Once she packed her clothes into a bag, and put the stuff that would not fit into her toy bag, both bags were stuffed. Trouble was, Robyn was done packing, but George was silent. So, she just stood there for a minute or two, before she got nervous, and said, 'Sir? Are you still there?"

"Yes I am slave, you need to learn patience. You are almost done, but you should change into something clean first. A pair of shorts and a tee shirt will be fine. No need for a bra or panties, you will be naked again once you get inside. Now find the clothes and get changed."

"Yes Sir, thank you Sir," she answered, actually relieved for that order, wearing the black dress in high heels in bright daylight felt so wrong.

She went to the closet and picked out a tee shirt, but George said, "Too loose, pick a tighter shirt."

"Yes Sir," she replied, and knew the one he would like. She pulled out a crop top tee that had the word 'BRAT' on the front. It was a size too small for her and barely covered her breasts.

As soon as she held it up, he said, "Perfect, you should have picked that first. Now I bet you have a pair of shorts that are too small for you too, not the sexy ones like you packed, just basic ones that don't quite fit you anymore."

Robyn remembered a pair she kept that she used to love, but became way too tight to wear in public, and too uncomfortable even around the house. She dug into a drawer and pulled them out, and once she unfolded them, he gave her his approval. Robyn would no longer feel weird in a black evening dress in bright daylight, instead, she would look like trailer trash. But there was no one around to see her, except maybe George, and looking like a cheap tart for him was fine.

There were three houses in the cul-de-sac, her parents' and George's were opposite each other's near the curved entrance road that concealed the court from the main road. The other house was at the back of the court, but it was completely hidden and had large metal gates at the end of the driveway. Robyn had seen some delivery trucks come by, but she never saw anyone around the gates, and it felt like it was a minor risk for her trek back to George's.

Once the shirt and shorts were on, she looked at her reflection and smiled at how her hard nipples were poking through her thin top's fabric. The shorts were another matter, they were so damn tight that she was afraid that the seams might split when she was lugging the bags and walking back to his house. She wondered if he would leave her to do it in bare feet, the black top roadway would be murder with the sun beating down on it.

She felt a sense of relief when he said, "Let me see what kinds of shoes you have slut."

"Yes Sir, thank you Sir, she replied, as she returned to the closet and looked down to the shoes lining the bottom.

As she scanned the large variety of footwear she had, he suddenly said, "The black ankle boots with the spiked heels looks good, put them on now, I want to see you in them.

"Yes Sir," she said, not surprised he picked something that would make walking difficult. But he also chose boots that would look ridiculous with the rest of her trashy attire.

She put them on, and stood in front of her dressing mirror thinking how sleazy she looked, and she heard him say, "Perfect, get that slutty body of mine back here pronto. Now move that tight little ass!"

"YES SIR!" she cried out, as she grabbed the backpack and slung it over her shoulders. Her tits nearly popped out of her top when she did, and she had to adjust the shirt, realizing a tit slip was possible if she had to carry the second bag, but it was a wheeled bag and she lifted the attached handle and rolled it out of her room and to the front door. She stepped outside, closed the door, but then he issued another command.

"Carry the second bag, no need to be lazy about it," George said, knowing that he would get a much better show that way.

"Yes Sir," she answered, not surprised that something she thought would be easy was made more difficult by him.

In order to keep her tits from popping out again, Robyn decided to use both arms to hold the handle in front of her body. That way she could use her arms to keep the girls under control, but she would look ridiculous with her legs banging against the suitcase with every step. Ludicrous or lascivious, it was an easy choice, though the latter was fine when she was with him. Once she picked it up, she started to march to the end of her driveway.

One thing she noticed was that the sun was hot and it was humid, so carrying two bags left her sweaty by the time she reached the end of her driveway. But then the worst thing possible happened when a delivery van pulled into the cul-de-sac and stopped right in front of her. Robyn was mortified when the passenger side window rolled down.

"Is this 2110 Barclay Court?" the driver asked, and Robyn put down the suitcase and pointed to the gated drive at the end of the court, not saying a thing. "Thanks, and hey, if you need a ride I would be happy to give you one."

"I bet you would, sorry my lesbian girlfriends are waiting for me, we are going to have an orgy," she replied with a little of her old self coming out from his suggestive offer.

"Bitch!" he snapped, and then he drove to the end of the court.

She grabbed her suitcase and waddled across the road as quickly as she could, wanting to get back into George's house before the delivery van passed by again. She breathed a sigh of relief when she reached his driveway, but she was only halfway up it when the van drove by again, with the driver beeping his horn and giving her the finger. She dropped the bag and started to turn, but a voice stopped her.

"What the fuck are you doing?"

It snapped Robyn out of her redheaded fury, and brought her back to reality, and she said, "Sorry Sir, he just pissed me off."

"Pick up the bag and get in here, now you are pissing me off," he said, and she realized that letting her old self out for that interaction with the delivery guy was a mistake. As she lugged her burden to the front door she wished she had just remained demure and polite, the bitchy side George just saw was the last thing he wanted from her. But it was true to her form, she let her emotions control her, acted without thinking, and now George would make her pay for it. It was another reminder that when she acted on her own, she usually got herself in big trouble.

When she reached the door, it opened and she saw George glaring at her, as he said, "Get your impertinent ass in here slut, you are in deep shit!" Robyn lumbered into the foyer and went to put the bag down, but he said, "Stop! Away for half an hour and you forgot the rules, so many mistakes in such a short time. Now you will stand there the way you are and think of the things you did wrong on your little trip. I'll be back."

He left her there, sweating profusely, and holding up all the weight in the bags was not making it any better. Robyn knew the obvious mistakes she made, but she feared he would find things that she missed. She had no idea what came over her out there, but he saw that side of her and she figured it would cause her plenty of trouble. It was a good reason to abandon her arrogant side, and she expected he would find a way to humble her. Something about that prospect suddenly seemed heartening.

CHAPTER 7: BASIC TRAINING

Robyn stood like a statue for over a half an hour before George returned and scowled at her again. She wanted to say she was sorry, but she knew he would make her feel her regrets, and that was probably better. She had realized that her naturally caustic personality was still there, only hidden by the submissive side that George had brought to light. But on her own for just a short walk across the street, she fell back into an old pattern and humiliated herself in his eyes. He wanted a demure woman, not a sassy and rude bitch.

"Well slave, you sure do know how to make a spectacle of yourself," he said.

"Yes Sir, I am sorry Sir," she said meekly.

"Put the bag down and take off the back pack," he said, and she eagerly obeyed. Once they were on the floor, he said, "Crawl behind me bitch, which is an appropriate name considering how I saw you treat that man."

"Yes Sir," Robyn said, as she dropped to the floor and followed him like his puppy.

He led her out to the patio, and since it was midday, the heat of the day was reaching its peak, and the humidity was oppressive too. She had almost cooled off inside the house, though holding up the one bag with the backpack slung over her shoulders never really let her body's heat dissipate. As soon as she crawled out onto the patio, even in the shade, the moist heat hit her hard all over again.

He led Robyn to the edge of the covered area of the patio, just ten feet from his swimming pool. She saw a wooden box on the concrete floor, probably two feet square, sitting under the edge of the roof. She looked upward and saw two leather cuffs hanging from short chains attached to the edge of the ceiling about five feet apart with the box sitting right between them. When he stopped so did she, but she was nervous, fearing what he planned.

So, when he said, "Stand on the box bitch," she knew what was coming, and though it was not a promising scenario, Robyn stood up and then she stepped up onto the box. It was a tad too high and she needed him to steady her until she could get both of her feet on the box, but the high heels on her boots left her precariously perched anyway. He stepped in front of her and she could still see him scowling, which worried Robyn.

He grabbed her left arm and lifted it up and outward, wrapping one cuff around her wrist and buckling it tightly. After the other wrist was cuffed, Robyn's arms were held up and angled outward above her head, but they were not carrying her weight, and her elbows were still partially bent. George moved back in front of her and stared at her for a few moments.

"The sassy bitch I saw acting so rudely to that driver is a problem, it is apparent that side of you is still looking to remain relevant. To become a slave, you need to learn some humility, and hanging out here for a while should teach you how to be a more humble creature, not such a bitchy one. Don't get me wrong, I love a challenge, and purging your impetuous nature will be fun for me, but likely not so much for you. Just remember, with me you will reap what you sow."

"Yes Sir," Robyn replied miserably. But it was not the impending punishment that upset her, it was how disappointed he sounded that made her heart ache. Why his moods affected her so strongly was still a mystery to Robyn, but it was becoming clear that she was not going to be happy when he was not.

"Think about what you want to be Robyn, my slave or a rude bitch," he said, and then he kicked the box out from under her feet.

"UHHHGGH!" Robyn groaned when her weight was taken by her arms and shoulders. The tips of her shoes were a few inches above the ground, leaving her unable to use her legs to ease the strain on her upper body. She was facing the pool, and as she began sweating profusely, Robyn realized that he left her facing the pool for a reason. Roasting in the heat with a pool just a few feet away from her, but inaccessible. It took very little time for her sparse top and tight shorts to become soaked in perspiration, sticking to her damp flesh, which made her feel even worse. Her feet in the leather boots felt like they were in a puddle, and overall, she was miserable in just fifteen minutes.

George was watching her hanging there limply, knowing that he was baking a lesson into her mind and body. She was far too pale skinned to stake her out on the lawn, as that was his first idea. He put Robyn in the shade hanging from the patio ceiling, absorbing the lesson in much the same way. The addition of suspending her created a similar stress that being under the beating rays of the sun would have also accomplished.

At the half hour mark, he activated her earbud, and said, "Are you still with me slut?"

"Yes Sir, please forgive me Sir. I will be good from now on, I promise Sir," she replied in a hoarse whisper.

"I am sure you think you will, but the way the bitch slipped out earlier tells me otherwise. Take some more time to consider your mistakes, and how you must atone for them. This may seem harsh, but it is for your own good."

"Yes Sir, thank you Sir," she replied dejectedly.

At the hour mark he could tell she had reached her limit, and he walked out onto the patio to stand facing her. Her head was bowed and he liked how she was so drenched in sweat that it was dripping off of her. Her eyes were closed and her breathing was ragged, which made him think that she was close to losing consciousness.

"Look at me slave," he said.

Robyn was deep in a fog, brought on by the strain on her body and how hot she felt, but she heard his voice cutting through it. She opened her eyes and lifted her slumped head to see him standing right in front of her. Her vision was blurry, but the fact that he was back gave her some hope that her punishment was nearly over. One thing she had learned was that he did not need to beat her to drive a point home, this kind of torment was slow and insidious, and it sent a clear message to the beleaguered girl.

When their eyes met, he said, "I think you have learned enough, would you like me to release you slave?"

"Yes Sir, please Sir! I promise to be a good slave," she answered, and even that was a strain that exhausted her.

He slid the box back under her feet, but she was barely able to use them to ease the strain on her arms and shoulders, as she was nearly worn out. Seeing how unstable she was made it trickier to release her wrists, but he managed. When the second cuff was removed, he actually had to catch her, as she crumpled into his arms. He laid her limp body on a chaise lounge and removed her boots, but he liked how her soaked shorts and top were plastered to her tits and crotch, so he left them alone.

After he plucked the earbud from her ear, he scooped her up again and carried her over to the pool. He saw the thermometer was reading over ninety degrees so he tossed her into it. She landed ass first, creating a large splash, and though the water wasn't cold, it was much cooler than her body. She was shocked, as the water overwhelmed her and she sank into it. But when her rump touched the bottom of the pool, it was like a switch went off, and she started flailing. Then she pushed herself up and popped out of the water.

She wiped the water from her eyes, now standing waist deep in the pool. When she cleared her vision, Robyn saw George standing at the edge of the pool with his arms folded. Though the immersion in the pool was a shock, Robyn realized that it woke her back up and she felt so much better than just a few minutes ago. She stared up at him in wonderment, not sure why the misery she was feeling was gone, and a renewed eagerness to serve this man now infused her.

"Give me your hand," he said, as he squatted and reached out toward her.

Robyn reached out, and once he grasped her hand, George yanked her out of the pool so fast that she almost fell into his arms again. But he kept her soaking wet body at arm's length. Before she even recovered from her rough removal from the pool, he used one hand to grab a clump of her soaked hair and used it to force her down to her knees. He tilted her head back, so she was facing up at him, and he could tell she was disoriented.

"That was part one of your punishment, and it cost you an hour of your chore time. Now you will dry off and put on your work outfit, what you need is over there," he said, pointing at the glass table. "When you are dressed, walk inside and I will give you the list of things you need to do before we make dinner. Tonight, I will give you part two before I send you home. Now get moving!" he snapped, as he released her hair and gave her a nice hard slap on the face.

"Yes Sir! Thank you Sir," she said, as she rubbed her stinging cheek. It wasn't a hard slap, and Robyn was surprised that she kind of liked it. Her bitchy side would have never tolerated a slap like that, but her new persona accepted that he was going to be rough with her, and it felt right.

He walked back into the house and left her again, so she got up and grabbed the towel that was folded neatly on the table. It was a big fluffy beach towel and after drying her face and hair with it, she put it down and peeled the shirt and shorts off of her damp body. Luckily the towel was bulky and absorbent enough to dry her whole body, after over an hour and a half bathed in sweat, Robyn finally felt at least partially normal again.

Since it was still hot and humid out on the patio, she quickly put on what he called an 'outfit.' What it really was, was the skimpiest bikini swimsuit she ever saw. It was black, but there was so little fabric that it looked more like a mass of strings. The bottom was a G-string with just a tiny triangular patch of cloth to cover her sex connected by strings. One of those strings was wedged in the crack of her ass, and basically left nothing to the imagination. The top was even skimpier, the string bra just had two triangular patches that she positioned over her erect nipples, which left her tits on full display. The last part of the ensemble was four inch high spike heeled pumps, which were hard to put on because they seemed too small for her.

But Robyn managed to get her feet into them. She stood up, and walked toward the door, wobbling a bit, as she had to adjust to walking on her toes again. She opened the door and appreciated the cool air conditioning waft over her skin, as she stepped inside and closed it behind her. She saw him sitting there in an armchair, but his face was obscured by a piece of paper he was holding, and presumably reading. She dropped to her knees and crawled over to him, and like a pet, she rubbed her head against one of his knees.

Without moving the paper, he said, "Stand up and let me see how you look."

Robyn got up and moved her hands behind her neck, linking her fingers together, and then arching her back, the way she had when she first stripped for him. It was less than a day ago, but to Robyn it felt awfully long ago, so much had happened since that moment. She also remembered the kiss he gave her before he tied her up and unleashed the latent slut inside her. Even though she masturbated almost every day, it was not until last night that she learned that she was a powerfully orgasmic girl. As she displayed her body for him again, she kind of hoped it would lead to another passionate escapade.

He put down the paper, and made a twirling gesture with his hand, as he perused her spinning around for him again. After few revolutions he said, "Stop and face me slave." Once she had stopped, he said, "This is the list of your chores for today. Normally you would be allotted three hours to complete them, but thanks to the bitchier side of you, you have only two. There is a closet over there with all you need, now get to work!" he said, while pointing to a narrow door on a wall.

She took the paper and said, "Yes Sir! Thank you Sir," before looking at the list, as she walked over to the closet.

By the time she reached the door, she saw she did have a lot of work to do, the kind she was used to having servants do for her. It was a stark reminder that she was not only surrendering to him, she was losing her privileged life too. Transitioning from a mean rich girl to a slave girl for George would certainly be a humbling experience, but he did say she needed to learn humility.

Scrubbing his toilets would certainly help her become a meeker person.

He had disappeared again, and she grabbed the cleaning supplies that were already in a carry tote, and Robyn headed upstairs, where the list started. After cleaning the two bathrooms upstairs, Robyn came to realize what hard work was really like. Dusting and vacuuming followed, and she found she was sweating again. Partly from the exertion, but also because she realized that she really did need three hours and there was no way she would finish his list in time.

She got through most of it, but the last few items were kitchen cleaning duties, and when she entered it, there he was sitting at the table. She put down her cleaning supplies, bowed her head, and began to sob. Her feet were aching in the tight shoes, her muscles were sore from all the work she did, and she really did feel chastened thanks to the experience.

"Did you get a good taste of how hard life can be slave?" he asked the weeping girl.

"Yes Sir, thank you Sir. I have been such a spoiled brat," she replied weepily.

"Yes you have, but you do not want to be one anymore, am I right?"

"Yes Sir."

He stood up, walked over to her, and then spun her around, turning her back to him. He wrapped his left around her throat and pulled her body against his, and her arms started to rise to resist before she stopped and dropped them to her sides. He then moved his right hand around her, placing his palm on her belly before sliding it down toward her sex. He smiled when she parted her legs as soon as his hand started moving, and her gasp of pleasure was music to his ears when his fingers reached her twat.

"If you want to feel me inside you someday soon, you had best not fuck up as badly as you did today slave. I can feel how wet you are slut, is your cunt as hungry as it feels?"

"Yes Sir, it is always wet around you," she cooed, as he was already making her knees weak the way he was playing with her pussy. She even liked the way his arm was pressing against her throat, she felt so controlled and, ironically, safe in his firm grip. After all he put her through this day, Robyn realized how powerful her attraction to him was, her old self would have bolted before any of this even started.

"Do you think you deserve an orgasm?" he asked, knowing it would confuse her.

She wanted to say yes, as she thought that such a rough day should earn her a reward, but she quickly discarded that thought. It came from her old selfish self, and he wanted her to become a gentler creature, one that knew her place as his slave. That meant she could not put her desires over his, and she sensed what he expected her to say.

So, she replied, "No Sir, I have been a naughty girl."

"And what does that mean slave?"

"I need more punishment Sir," she replied, but not sadly, this time it sounded very sexy.

"And you have made this decision on your own?" he replied.

Realizing her mistake, Robyn replied, "I'm sorry Sir, I just thought that was what you told me yesterday, naughty girls need punishment."

"You really do have a lot to learn, first you tell me what I should do, and then you make a lame excuse about why you did. You are lucky that I like a challenge, but at this point the discipline session I have planned for after dinner will not address all your infractions from today. But we will eat first, so be quiet before you get in more trouble" he said, as he released his grip on her and spun her back around to face him.

Then he gripped Robyn under her armpits and lifted her up off the floor. He carried her over to the marble topped island and sat her warm rump on the cool stone. Robyn gasped when her buns met the marble, but it was the way he just grabbed her and placed her here that had the biggest impact on her. He was so damn domineering and masculine, and it was appealing to her like nothing else never had. She used to scoff at the jocks and macho guys, but George was like a Nordic god, and she was beginning to adore him.

From her new perch she saw two delicious looking steaks sitting on the counter and she watched him start a burner under a cast iron frying pan. He explained to her how to make a steak to his liking, and though she wished she could take notes, she just watched and listened intently. For a girl who was easily bored, Robyn was determined to learn to cook for him, and the smell of the steak made that desire even stronger.

He also gave her a tour of his cabinets, so she would know where everything was. She took it all in, as she felt that he was basically domesticating her. First cleaning, then cooking, laundry was probably next! But sitting there next to naked in his kitchen watching him cooking steaks told her that it was much more than that. Whatever he planned for after dinner was at the back of her mind and that was what made this so alluring. She was actually looking forward to the next punishment, even after the awful one on the patio. Something about the way he made her feel when he was being cruel to her made her want to please him even more. It made no sense, but none of this did. Part of her thought she would eventually wake up and it would all be a dream, but the rest of her wanted this to be real.

Dinner was a devilishly erotic adventure for Robyn, as she knelt on a cushion on the floor next to George's seat. Her arms were folded behind her back and he fed her pieces of meat with his fingers, which she had to suck clean before chewing her food. Then she had to chew exactly twenty five times before swallowing and opening her mouth to await the next piece. It was almost as kinky as her appetizer was, because she had leaked all over his island and had to lick it up before crawling to the table for her supper.

After dinner she finished the last part of her chore list, and the hour it took left her anxious about what he was planning next. But the worst part for Robyn was that an impending punishment did not quell her sexual appetite, which had not been fed a scrap for the whole day. He said she was not ready to fuck him, but now she wondering if he would also deny her the kind of pleasure that knocked her out cold last night. She could see him doing that, and apart for a tiny tease just before dinner, her prospects for more pleasure were looking rather dim.

When she was finally finished, Robyn went to the study, as he told her to do before he left her to finish her chores. When she reached the door she dropped to her knees and crawled into the room, liking how it felt to slink around like an animal in his presence. It reminded her that she had accepted a role that made her inferior, and around him she did feel that way. He knew everything she had been up to; he had read her like a cheap book. Ever since he put her over his knee, Robyn felt like he was the one to finally make her pay the price for her selfish disposition.

When he saw her crawling over to him, George said, "Lose the bikini and climb up on the ottoman where you will kneel facing me."

Robyn scurried over to the ottoman and gladly disposed of her minimal bikini before assuming her specified position. She wished he told her to take off her tight shoes too, but he did not, so they remained on as she knelt on the footrest. He told her to spread her knees and keep her feet together, and once Robyn did, he had her fold her arms behind her back.

Then he said, "Well Robyn, it has been just about a day since you chose to follow me, are you still committed to remaining on the path to becoming my slave?"

Robyn looked at him, confused that he asked her that question. She had already told him that she wanted him to train her, and now she wondered if he was changing his mind. Just as she was getting used to the idea of him making all the decisions, he was asking her to make one again. She definitely wanted more of this and him, so it was easy to say what she did.

"Yes Sir, I know I need you to show me how to embrace my submissive side and purge the brat once and for all."

"Very well, but after that episode in the roadway today, I learned that the brat is still a part of you, hiding just below the surface. Extreme discipline will eventually dispel it, but before I embark on that course I must test your mental fortitude. For your first week in training, I will test your ability to comply without the benefits you will get once you prove your determination to become what I want. Simply put, receiving sexual pleasure is banned until you show me that you can perform without the benefit of sexual release. Are you prepared to accept those terms?"

"Yes Sir," she answered, even though he just confirmed what she was worried about, but she reminded herself that it was only temporary. If she showed him how obedient she was, that which he just denied her would be granted, and that goal was all that mattered to her.

CHAPTER 8: HIS BOOK OF RULES

Robyn saw him pick up a folder from a small table beside his chair, and as he held it up, he said, "This is now your responsibility, the rules that I expect you will follow to the letter. And rather than giving you a physical punishment tonight, I will send you back to your parents' house to read and memorize your rules. But, before I send you on your way, I have something special for you to wear during your time away from me."

Then he held up a metal device that made Robyn go wide-eyed. Given the shape of it, she guessed it was some sort of chastity belt. He had said she was not allowed to orgasm, and if her sex was hidden behind this thing that looked like oversized metal panties, that order would be impossible to break. As he held it up for her to see, she cringed when she noticed the two small metal shafts mounted inside the gusset, realizing where they would spend the night.

After showing it to her, he said, "Yes slave, this is a chastity belt with a couple of interesting enhancements. It will make it impossible for you to play with yourself. I will be monitoring you with these things too," as he held up her earbud and her smart phone. He found it in her purse she left behind from the date they had, and with his tech skills, he easily hacked and modified it.

As Robyn tried to digest all he was throwing at her, he also said, "You will now go and use the bathroom, because once this goes on, it does not come off until you return tomorrow morning. You may walk to the bathroom now and do your business, now get moving."

Robyn scurried off to do what he wanted. She was frustrated and confused, she had braced herself for another punishment, never imagining that tonight he would just send her packing in a chastity belt to stew in her own juices. But by the time she finished peeing and cleaning up down there, she realized that what he said earlier about testing her 'mental fortitude' became clearer. Denying her what she craved and making her focus on him and the rules he wanted her to learn.

When she returned, he had her stand in front of him, while he knelt down and installed the chastity belt. The three inch wide metal waist band had slots on one side and a D-ring on the other, so he was able to adjust it to fit securely to her waist just above her hip bones. Then she watched him lubricate the two metal shafts in the gusset section, glad that they were relatively small. Once they were greased, he pulled the piece forward in between her legs from where it was attached to the back of the waistband.

Robyn cringed when the cold slick intruder easily breached her sphincter, and she reacted the same way when the other one climbed into her sex. The crotch piece aligned with the D-ring that linked the waistband together, and she watched him secure both parts with a single tiny padlock. He had her walk around the room in it. She found that, apart from the way the 'enhancements' were wiggling around inside her rectum and pussy, it was fairly comfortable. Seeing that the lock was in front made it clear that it was there to remind her that she could not remove it.

Once he was satisfied that the belt was properly fitted, he said, "Now let's get you dressed."

He retrieved one of the dresses she brought over earlier, the least sexy of them all, and one she was surprised he wanted. Now she knew why, it was loose fitting and would hide the metal belt from view. It did have an elastic section just below her breasts, which made them look more prominent, but below that it was pleated and loose. It did have a hem that ended at mid-thigh, so bending over might be somewhat challenging and she hoped she would not face that situation.

Of course, she was also left braless, and when she walked around in the dress, her breasts visibly bounced in the crepe like fabric that enclosed them. It also left her prominently erect nipples poking against it, plainly visible through the thin fabric. None of that really bothered her at this point, Robyn was finding that looking sexy to the point of being sleazy actually excited her in a way she never imagined possible. So far, everything he had done with her was so far out of the normal sphere of reality that her mind was still trying to process it all and why it excited her.

Once he fitted the bud back in her ear and tested it, he handed her the phone. I have disabled most of the phone functions, the only phone you will be able to send or receive texts from is mine. I may text you, or use the earbud, so you best keep the phone handy. Once you get back to your place, go directly to your room and lock yourself in it. I will provide further instructions at that point," he said, as he handed her the purse she had with her from their date.

"Yes Sir, I will miss you Sir," Robyn said sadly, not really wanting to go home at all.

"That is good slave, you should miss me when I am not with you. But, it will also help you to appreciate me even more, what do they say? Absence makes the heart grow fonder? I think that's it," he said, as he led her to his front door for another trip into her past. But the chastity belt she was wearing reminded her that there was something very different about it this time.

As Robyn walked across the street, she realized how bad her feet ached in the tight pumps she had been wearing for hours now. She hoped that he would let her take them off when she got to her room, and if he did not, she planned on asking him if she could. She remembered the coffee fiasco from this morning, and hoped that asking his permission for some things might be acceptable, but she still wasn't sure. She had never been this confused in all her life.

Since it was dark out, and there was no one around during her walk, it went much smoother than it did when she was returning to his place earlier that day. She saw neither Rose nor Albert, her parents' servants, when she entered the house. She just made a quick dash for her room. Once she was inside and the door was locked, she stood there waiting for his next instruction. As she waited, fairly certain that he was testing her patience, Robyn looked around the room and realized that she no longer liked it, or wanted to be here any longer. She began hoping that he would move her into his place sooner rather than later.

After a few minutes her phone chimed and she looked at it. It said, 'Take off the dress and shoes and then get in bed with your folder.'

Robyn immediately kicked the shoes off her feet, and then pulled the dress off before taking her phone and folder and jumping into her bed. As soon as she was sitting up with her pillows propped up behind her, the next message told her to read through the whole folder and, when she was done, she could text him any questions she had about it. It sounded simple enough, at least until she started reading it.

The first paragraph spelled out the agreement she had to make with him, he would make all the decisions and she would follow his direction without question. Nothing in the first paragraph was new to her, he had told her as much, but it was now on paper and Robyn expected that he would want her to recite it verbatim at some point.

It was what came next that was an eye opener. A torrent of rules that basically left only breathing out of the things she would need permission to do. Everything from waking to sleeping would be under his direction with a whole lot of kinky rituals she would have to perform in between. He had a list of short commands that spelled out particular positions for her to assume, and the descriptions of some of them got her all hot and bothered. The first part spelled out all the mundane duties of her slavery, but when she got to the next part, she found quite a few things that made her very nervous.

In the section marked, 'Personal Hygiene,' Robyn just stared at the page when it said she would give herself a daily enema, *more if needed*. She had never even had an enema, let alone giving herself one, and every day? Then she saw the notation that more would be explained in the anal play section. The idea of anal play did not alleviate her nerves, it just amplified them. The various forms of punishments he laid out made her head spin, some of them sounded kind of sexy, but others were downright creepy. At least he promised no scarring, maiming, or major physical damage, but the many ways he described to inflict pain on her almost seemed unbelievable.

The more Robyn read, the more she began to think that maybe he was trying scare her away. But despite all the cruel and invasive things she read, her sex got all wet and sloppy again. It was even worse when she noticed that she was flexing her vaginal and anal muscles against the steel shafts nestled inside her holes. She was scared, but she was still as horny, or maybe hornier, than ever. She was beginning to think she was deranged, how could all the cruel and downright evil things he planned for her make her so hot? Since she always followed her instincts, she went with her carnal desires, and she fully expected it would cause her a whole lot more trouble.

The last part gave her some optimism, it seemed that he intended to move her into his place in a week if she met his expectations in her initial training. They would concoct an excuse for her to tell Rose and Albert that she was going away to spend some time with friends for a few weeks. If at the end of that period he was satisfied with her, he would consider a permanent arrangement. It was all so bizarre, having barely known him for a day and he was already proposing permanently enslaving her.

As she finished reading the material he gave her, Robyn realized that this was something that could have lifelong repercussions. At dinner he told her that this was the time for her to go out and explore, but what she read was more like a blueprint for being cut off from the real world. She did realize that his proposal was also a map to a different kind of exploration. Even though she would have to abandon the normal world, she would be learning about a much darker one. Given the way her body was reacting, as she pondered the myriad ways he planned on testing her mettle, Robyn still felt the urge to take this deviant path. If she did not, she was pretty sure she would eventually regret not exploring these new feelings that were pervading her body and thoughts.

Since she expected that he was monitoring her, Robyn closed the folder and asked, "Sir? Are you there?"

After a few moments, she heard him in her ear, as he said, "Well Robyn, does my proposal scare you, or does it entice you?"

Her answer was simple, as she replied, "Both Sir, you expect a lot from a slave."

"No Robyn, I expect everything. To become my slave, you will have to surrender all you are to become all I want. If you were not scared I would be surprised, but the question you have to answer is simple. Are you willing to face your fears and trust that I will show you a way to live that speaks to your soul? You have only spent one day with me so far, but I think you feel the kind of chemistry we share, am I right?"

"Yes Sir," she replied, as that was not in question.

"I do too, and I will make this a little easier. As I have set out a time line to follow, I will allow you the chance to back out after the first week of training. If you instead choose to move in after this week, you will get another chance to bow out after a month of living with me if you do not want to commit to something permanent. So, now that you know that you will have two more chances to end this, does that make it easier to explore the adventure I have proposed?"

"I am really scared Sir, some of the things you expect just sound cruel," she admitted, wanting him to know that she had deep misgivings.

"Let me ask you a question. Did reading my proposal also arouse you?"

"Yes Sir."

"So, like anything in life, you must weigh the pros and cons. Is your fear stronger than your desire? Are you strong enough to face the uncertainty and explore those desires? Remember that I just offered you two more chances to back out and go back to where you were before you brought that piece of mail to me yesterday, so, nothing is set in stone yet. If this is not what you really want, I am sure that in the next few weeks you will know for sure. Take the night to sleep on it, and in the morning you can decide if you want to take the next step."

"Yes Sir, thank you Sir," she replied, and then she asked, "What time should I set my alarm clock?"

Robyn gasped when she felt the shafts nestled inside her body start vibrating, and she heard him say, "I will wake you up when it is time."

Robyn cooed, "Yesss Sir," as the damn things took her breath away, and her simmering arousal spiked once again.

George shut it down before it could really stoke her up, but it did leave her panting like a thirsty dog. Her head was swirling again, and she heard him say, "Sleep well Robyn, you will need all your energy for tomorrow."

She put the folder on her nightstand and laid down, and then she said, "Yes Sir, thank you Sir." That little buzz left her feeling relaxed, and a little frustrated. He had quelled her biggest fears, giving her the chance to opt out if this if it became too much for her to handle. But she had another worry, and that was based on how powerful her sex drive was becoming because of these kinky games. She wondered if weeks of swimming in the deep end of submission would become an addiction. And if it did, would she have enough will power to decide if what she had to sacrifice for it was really worth the price she would pay?

The last day had been so tumultuous that it ultimately left Robyn extremely tired, and after their conversation, sleep came quickly. Her dreams that night, ones she would remember in the morning, helped make her decision for her. She saw herself bound, whipped, and best of all, fucked by George, and it was wonderful. When she was awakened by powerful vibrations in her anal tract, as he chose not to activate the vaginal prod. Robyn sat up and loudly said, "Good morning Sir!"

The vibrations stopped, and then he said, "Good morning Robyn. Time to decide if you want this to continue, do you want to come to me to start your training?"

It took her no time to answer, and she said, "Yes Sir, please Sir!"

"Then you may go to the bathroom and wash up, and when you get back we will pick the outfit you will wear today," he said.

Robyn had to admit that she liked the way he ordered her around, once again reminded that letting him direct her actions felt right. Maybe not in the normal sense and not the way most people would look at it, but to her it was intoxicating. She had always been independent and a bit of a contrarian, if someone said 'left' she invariably would think 'right.' It was starting to dawn on her that she had not really changed at all, and this was attractive to her primarily because it was not what most people would choose.

Then there was the little matter of how erotic this all felt, even though she had experimented with her sexuality a lot in the last year, what happened in the last day made it all seem so petty and ineffective. Remembering how he tied her up and sent her into orbit with sexual ecstasy demanded that she explore this strangely deviant form of sexual satisfaction. By the time she finished in the bathroom, Robyn was eager to get dressed and get back to him.

As she entered her bedroom from the ensuite bath, he said, "Go to the closet and I will pick out an outfit for you."

She was both relieved and disappointed, as she liked dressing sexily for him. But the way he made her dress just to cross the street had a lot to do with her confrontation with the delivery man yesterday. She knew she should have handled it better, but his decision suggested that her return to his place would be much easier today. Once she opened the closet and went through some of her clothes, he picked a jogging outfit. A light blue pair of sweat pants and a matching jacket, but that was it, he told her the jacket was all she would wear as a top.

Once she put them on, he said, "The jacket's zipper is too high, pull it down to just below your tits slave."

"Yes Sir," she replied, as she pulled the zipper down to where he wanted it. Looking at her reflection she saw how her breasts and cleavage were now exposed, not totally, but enough to add some sleaze to a generally boring outfit. She smiled when he told her that she looked much better that way, and after he picked a pair of her running shoes for her to wear, she was almost ready to go. He then made her collect and bag her sexiest shoes and swimsuits this time, as he had left them out of yesterday's wardrobe transfer. Once she had her bag, her rule book, and her phone in hand, he told her to come to him.

Robyn left her room, hoping to avoid Rose and Albert, as she could hear they were in the kitchen. But, as she reached the bottom of the steps, his voice stopped her again. "Will they be suspicious if you don't tell them you are going out?"

"No sir, they would be suspicious if I did, I always ignore them," she replied quietly.

"Fine, then you may proceed."

"Thank you Sir," Robyn replied, as she carefully moved to the front door and exited the house as stealthily as she could. She nearly started running, but he told her to slow down before she reached the end of her driveway. She immediately stopped jogging and just briskly walked across the road and onto his property. Even though she knew that once she was with him that she would face a difficult day, she wanted to be with him so badly that her fears could not deter her.

When she reached the door she stopped and waited, knowing that ringing the bell or a knock on the door was unnecessary. He knew she was here and would let her in when he chose to, and it surprised her that she was beginning to understand George, just not quite as well as he knew her. The door opened and he told her to enter, and once she did, he slammed it closed.

He had spelled out what she needed to do in her rule book, so Robyn put the bag on the floor and stripped off the clothes and shoes, just leaving the locked chastity belt in place. Then she knelt on the floor facing him, doing her best to assume the position the way he had spelled it out for her. He looked down at her for a few moments before picking up her clothes, shoes, and the bag. Then he began to walk away, but he also said something.

"Prostrate yourself."

Robyn immediately laid down on her belly and spread her arms and legs outward, assuming the position the way it was described in the rule book. She stayed like that for a few minutes before he returned, but all she could see were his bare feet in front of her face. She ached for her next command, finding that the way he left her waiting was somehow fueling her need to perform for him. Looking at his bare toes, she wondered what he planned for her next.

"A good slave will be happy to kiss her owner's feet, kiss mine slave Robyn," he said.

She eagerly obeyed, feeling like his slave, as she kissed and licked his toes. But it was something he said that made her belly churn, when he referred to the fact that a slave was *owned,* and that notion was tempting to her. He intended to own her! It made her feel special, George just let her know that his goal was to possess her! As draconian as that sounded, it still attracted her, though her old self would have surely balked. She was always proud of her ability to make her own choices, but now she wanted him to take on that role, and that was what really surprised her.

After a few minutes of groveling at his feet, George said, "Crawl behind me slave, time to get you out of that belt so you can clean yourself out."

As Robyn crawled behind him, she had a pretty good idea what he meant. He led her up to his room, and then into the master bath. She saw the enema bag hanging from the showerhead on the wall in the large stall. There was also a small stool sitting on the floor of the shower, and she cringed at the thought of getting her bowels flushed out. Since she knew this was coming from her bedtime reading last night, she was kind of glad, fearing that she might have freaked out if he dropped this on her without warning. In fact, much of the harsh treatment he had planned for her was spelled out in the book of rules he gave her. This was just one of the many ways he planned to turn her into his submissive plaything.

He had her stand up, as he unlocked and removed her chastity belt. Then he said, "In you go slave, kneel and bend over the stool, facing away from the enema bag."

It was not like his intentions were not clear, and as she assumed the position, she was trying to brace herself for what was coming. Once she was in position, he said, "Take this and stick it up your ass," handing her the enema nozzle.

As she took it, Robyn did not like the look of the bulbous part in the middle of the plastic outlet. She did not realize that it was not a 'normal' nozzle at all, as she never had seen an enema bag and hose. That bulge was not part of a standard nozzle, and though she was glad the end was much narrower, she dreaded forcing the bigger section through her butt hole.

But Robyn felt a strong compulsion to obey when he gave her orders, so she thanked him and she took it. Then she proceeded to clumsily insert it into her ass. She groaned when it started to stretch her sphincter open, but she moaned sexily when it popped into her hole. Once again, Robyn found her predicted fear was exaggerated and what he made her do was not too hard at all. But she had yet to feel the fluid flowing into her colon, and she was edgy, just maybe a little less.

She saw him place a stool on the shower floor in front of her, and she also noticed that he was now as naked as she was! When he took a seat on the stool facing her, the sight of his erection made her pussy twitch. He reached over her back and snatched the extra-long enema hose he chose. He had planned this out and needed a tube long enough so that when he opened the clip holding the fluid back, he would do it while sitting in front of Robyn.

But there was another reason, which became apparent when he said, "Suck my cock slut."

"Yes Sir!" she answered. Then she bent her head down and took his staff between her lips.

As she went to town on his rod, George fingered the clip that would start emptying the bag into her colon. He was waiting for her to get really into what she was doing. Then, when he thought she was nice and worked up, making such sexy slurping sounds around his cock, he unleashed the enema. Her moans suddenly became sharper and deeper, and he could feel her trembling.

"Relax slave, let it flow as you suck, focus on the cock in your mouth and nothing else," he said as he gently stroked her bobbing head.

Robyn did not like the enema one little bit, but he was diabolical in the way that he got her all distracted giving him a blow job before he started it. If his cock was not occupying her mouth she would have likely whined and cried throughout it. Instead, as much as she disliked the feeling in her bowels, the cock in her mouth was making her sex throb. The opposing forces almost cancelled each other out, but it was more like her budding sexual appetite was overpowering any other feelings she was experiencing.

Robyn tried to stay focused on the cock in her mouth, but as the bag emptied and her bowels filled, the cramps began. It was awful, and as her moaning turned to whining it was not lost on George. Just as she reached the point that she thought she could take no more, the flow slowed and soon afterward it stopped. She never had such a strong urge to shit as she did in that moment, and she hoped he would pull the plug out of her ass so she could expel the fluid churning inside her.

He said, "Stop sucking and I will remove the plug slave."

Robyn released her oral grip on his shaft, and she said, "Yes...Sir...thank...you...Sir!" clearly struggling to get the words out.

George got up and left the shower, taking his stool with him. Robyn was whining loudly, her poor belly feeling achingly bloated, which was exacerbated because of the way she was bent over the stool. George moved behind her, and before removing the nozzle from her anus, he turned on the shower. It startled her, but George had an on demand hot water system, and it went from chilly to nice and warm before he could reach down and pull the nozzle from her anus.

When he did tug the spout from her ass, Robyn screamed, "Thank you Sir!" as she felt the relief of squirting out the fetid fluid from her bowels. It was awful smelling, even with the shower water pouring down her back that helped dilute it and send it down the shower drain. But, as she was pushing it out, she felt his fingers reaching under her to caress her clit. When that started, she found that her anus began squirting harder, as her body reacted to the clitoral stimulation by making her vaginal muscles flex. As the relief from expelling the enema gripped her, so did her arousal from his digital attention.

112

"That's a good slave, push it all out," he said soothingly, and the tone of his voice coupled with the way he was stroking her clit was flipping the script. Robyn's torturous enema was turning into another highly charged erotic event. Her mind, which had been revolting during the enema, was thrown into another potential orgasmic release. But, when her anal expulsion turned from a stream to a trickle, he removed his hand. That left Robyn panting in frustration, and since she was told she could not climax, she was also left disappointed.

Finally, he took the shower wand and rinsed her back with it before aiming it her crotch, both rinsing her backside and making her squirm in arousal. When he was done rinsing her he said, "Time to get to work slave."

CHAPTER 9: A DAY OF HARSH LESSONS

After Robyn got out of the shower and dried off with the towel George gave her, he handed her a new list of chores. This time all she was given to wear while performing her duties was another pair of tight fitting high heels. Her first task was to make George breakfast, and he stood there directing her every step of the way. Apart from the fact that she was stark naked, she kind of felt like she was becoming his woman, and found that she liked cooking for him.

Eating her breakfast, on the other hand, was even more demeaning than yesterday. He put her plate on the floor next to his chair, and she had to eat it on her hands and knees, just like a pet dog. As a reward for cleaning her plate, she had the privilege of finishing the blowjob she started in the shower, since he had not climaxed. This time he gave her a nice bellyful of his spunk, and she contentedly swallowed every drop, even though she still ached to feel his dick filling her sex.

After she drained him, he made her bend over the table while he teased her close to another orgasm. But when she begged for permission to climax, as it was spelled out in the rule book, he stopped and slapped her ass a few times. Then he said, "Here is today's list of chores, I will be working in the study while you perform them."

Robin took the list and replied, "Yes Sir," once again frustrated by his teasing. And what made it worse was that she got so close this time. She guessed his intent; while he denied her sexual release, he was going to keep her horny. It was another fiendish aspect of his method of training that she feared would drive her crazy. As she went to perform her duties, Robyn also feared that when he finally granted her the right to experience the incendiary sexual release he was currently denying her, it would be so appealing that she would become putty in his hands.

Once the breakfast dishes were done, she found today's list was different than the one from yesterday. It did not really matter, in fact, doing a different set of chores was like a new adventure for a girl who barely toiled at anything before she met him. It took almost four hours to get through the whole list, and she meekly entered the study when it was done. She was tired and sweaty, doing menial tasks like cleaning took an awful lot of effort. Her sense of entitlement was quickly eroding, as the reality of true servitude was beginning to sink into her mind.

When Robyn crawled up to him, he surprised her by feeding her some fruit while she knelt beside him. Then he pointed to a large dog bed and told her to take a nap until he finished working and he had time to give her further training. Even though curling up on a pet bed was demeaning, she was glad to nap on the floor next to him. The chores had really exhausted her. She stared at him working on his laptop, wondering why she was so easily falling under his sway. But as she closed her eyes to nap, she discarded those thoughts, fearing they might create doubts. She was already aching for her next sexual adventure, and she knew that to get it she had to show him she could be a good slave. And oddly enough, she really wanted to prove it to herself too.

He allowed Robyn a two hour nap, mainly because he had to finish ordering some special equipment so he would have it before he moved her into his house. Looking at the naked nymph sleeping on the floor, just like his pet, renewed his desire to totally captivate her. She was already amazingly obedient and was performing much better than he ever expected. It figured that all the searching he did was futile, and that he found the best candidate yet living just across the street. He knew she was not there yet, and could balk if he pushed her too far or too fast.

Still, Robyn had already had many of the earmarks of a true submissive. It also helped that they had a powerful chemistry between each other. He was fairly certain that she was far more smitten with him at this point, why else would she agree to his shameful demands? During their dinner date he noticed how she spoke of her history in a very independent way, while her manner with him was much more deferential. He sensed she might be using bravado to mask a submissive nature, and the way he had played her, he was pretty sure he was right in that assessment.

Then there was her incredible libido, he was still amazed how she had climaxed when he gently slapped her pussy. It seemed that she might also be a masochist, and if so, that opened up a whole array of games most women could not handle. He knew he would have to test that theory before he took the leap and moved her in, but it would mean giving her something he told her that she was denied. But, since it would be tied to a painful experience, he thought up a devious way to test his theory and make her think that she had just failed to follow his orders.

Since it was midafternoon. and he doubted she would be very focused after he executed his next escapade, he decided to wake her and prep the food for their dinner before he played with her. He roused her by prodding one of his feet into the soft malleable flesh of her tits, and when her eyes opened, she smiled brightly up at him. He returned the gesture and moved his foot up to her lips, and without a verbal command, she kissed it.

As she worshipped his toes with her lips, he said, "We will be doing some dinner prep next, and when we are done, I will address more of your mistakes before we eat," and then he pulled his foot away, and added, "You may walk behind me."

"Yes Sir, thank you Sir," she replied, as she scrambled to her feet and followed behind him to the kitchen.

He tapped the island in the same spot where she sat the day before and she took his cue to hop up onto it again. He pulled a pair of large chicken breasts from the fridge, and then began to prepare them for baking. He started explaining what he was doing, and she took a risk and asked, "Sir? Can I ask a favor?"

"What do you want?" he asked, sounding mildly annoyed.

"If I could take notes it will help me when you want me to start cooking for you on my own," she answered quite meekly, having sensed his testy mood.

He spun around and looked at her for a moment, and then he smiled and said, "That is a favor I will be happy to grant, you have a very good point." Then he pulled a pad and pen from a drawer and handed them to her.

"Thank you Sir," she said, as she quickly wrote down what he already did, and then she took thorough notes as he got the food ready.

When he slipped it into the oven, giving them an hour before it would be ready, he said, "Put the pad and pen back in the drawer, but you can get it out every time I teach you a new recipe." Then, once she did, he said, "It's play time slave, get down on your hands and knees and crawl to the study. I will meet you there momentarily."

"Yes Sir, thank you Sir," she replied, as she eagerly obeyed his command.

Robyn crawled to the room and knelt beside his chair when she got there, it seemed like it was an appropriate place to wait for him. When she heard him enter the room from behind her, she did not even look over her shoulder, content to wait for his next command before she did a thing. It was so bizarre feeling the need to wait for him to direct her, but the more she did it, the more Robyn liked being under his control. It was so much simpler, and so far, exhilarating. He came up to her and dumped some things onto the empty chair, and though she wanted to look at what they were, she stared down at her tits instead. That was the other aspect of this relationship that surprised her, he kept her naked and she liked it! Robyn

118

had been a relatively modest person, with her body at least. But running around his house buck naked gave her a kind of thrill that she never expected. Pretty much everything that happened with George had a strange and exotic air about it.

"Face down on the ottoman with your ass pointed at the chair!" George barked, and he smiled when she scrambled into position.

He spread and roped her knees to the two feet closest to his chair, creating a perfect view of her ass and pussy. Then, he roped her elbows together and secured them to the ottoman's feet on the opposite side, leaving her on her elbows and facing down at the floor. He took the last items off the chair and sat in it, enjoying the view of Robyn's rump with her sex winking at him just below it. He took a look at the tools he would use to really confuse her, a paddle and a vibrator.

He said, "You have not yet made up for yesterday's infractions, but now you will. The bare handed spanking you got was more of a test to see if it aroused you. Since it did, today I will give you your first taste of the paddle. The rules are the same, are you ready to begin?"

"Yes Sir, thank you Sir," she replied nervously. She was pretty sure that her first spanking would seem mild compared to today's and she hoped that she could handle it.

She heard the loud swish and the loud crack against her right butt cheek, and after a short shriek, she cried out, "Thank You SIR! May I have another?" The second strike came as soon as she was done, and it knocked the breath out of her when her left cheek took its first blow. She managed to say her part again, but it felt like her rump hurt as much now as it had after her entire hand spanking. How she could handle more was an open question, she was already thinking of begging for mercy.

But then he threw her a curveball, as he turned on the vibrator and pressed it against her clit. Robyn shrieked again, as she lurched forward instinctually trying to avoid the intense feeling exploding from her clit. It only lasted a little while, ten seconds to be exact. But it was enough to calm her down and make sure he did not beat the passion out of her. When she thanked him once she caught her breath, George was gaining confidence about how he was maneuvering her.

The next round got her two whacks per cheek before she got a fifteen second buzz on her clit. While her rump was becoming red-hot, so was her sex drive. She silently cursed him, even while she thanked him, sensing how this roller coaster ride from pain to pleasure was twisting her mind into knots. It hurt so bad, but she almost climaxed both times he teased her with the vibrator. It made no sense, and the overflow of sensations was making it harder to think at all.

Round three brought three whacks to each side of her rump, he was avoiding the middle so that the chastity belt Robyn would wear to bed would not irritate any beaten flesh. She was still so raw and untrained, he decided to carefully mete out the pain, to slowly coax out the masochist that he suspected was lurking inside Robyn. And after the six total swats, she received a twenty second clitoral assault that pushed her even closer to an orgasm.

She was trembling and panting heavily after he pulled the vibrator away from her twat the third time. But it was how wet and twitchy he left her cunt that made George smile. He could tell that his plan was working, as the sides of her ass cheeks were dark red and starting to bruise, yet she was still on the verge of a climax. It was a very good indicator of a potential pain slut. And if she was really that kinky, then he knew he hit submissive gold!

This last round would be very revealing if it went the way he planned, so he started with the final swats, four per side for a grand total of ten per cheek. Her last few thanks and subsequent requests for more became hoarse whispers, as her voice became weak and ragged. She was crying freely by that point, and George knew she was miserable. It was time to see if he could flip the script and send her in another direction.

Robyn was immersed in the worst pain she ever felt, weeping and wondering why she chose to accept this kind of cruel treatment. But then he pushed the vibrator against her sex again and since her clit was already primed and ready, those sensations overwhelmed the pain. She began to shudder, realizing she was heading into another sexual maelstrom. Even though thinking was a challenge, she remembered one of her rules and struggled to find her voice.

"PLEASE SIR! Please let me come!" she bellowed, hoping against hope that he would let her reach orgasm this time.

Knowing she was just about at the point of no return, he said, "No, I told you the rules!"

"But! BUT! BUT!!!" Robyn screamed, as the orgasm happened anyway, and she was plunged into an explosion of sexual satisfaction. It buried the pain radiating from her rump, as her sex went wild and she could do nothing to stop it.

"Naughty slut, it sure looks like you are climaxing," he said mockingly.

"Yesss Sirrr, sssorry Sirrr," Robin growled, enjoying the incredible sensations assailing her while also worrying about how angry this was making him.

He pulled the vibrator away and loved how her sex was visibly throbbing, now knowing that he could intertwine pain and pleasure with Robyn to achieve devastating results. Watching her body shudder and twitch for several minutes after he pulled the vibrator off her sex was a sight to behold, one that opened up so many possibilities for George and his sadistic appetites. Once she settled down, it was time to enhance the bond even further.

George stood up, dropped his pants, and then walked around the bound girl to kneel with his hard dick pointing at her head, which was currently bowed downward. He grabbed a clump of her curly ginger locks and lifted her head up until she faced up at him. Her eyes took a moment to focus on his, as he stared down at her with a stern look on his face.

"You handled the punishment well, but failed the test of self-control by having an orgasm. So, now you will return the favor, open up your hot mouth slut," he said, as he used his other hand to hold his dick and slap it against her chin.

"Yes Sir, thank you Sir," Robyn answered, and then she opened her mouth.

As he slipped it between her lips, Robyn was more confused than ever. The sides of her buttocks were hurting badly, but her sex was still twitching happily. She had to wonder how such brutal pain disappeared when her sex was buzzed into orgasm, it made no sense. Then again, nothing in George's world adhered to logic or reason. It was its own a bizarre reality, where up meant down and pain led to pleasure.

He was surprised how voraciously she was sucking his cock, looking down at her rump he could see she would sport some bruises for a few days. After such a painful paddling she could have retreated into her mind, but the way she was working his dick showed she was still with him. Even though he blew a load earlier that day, and could have milked this blowjob for a while, having watched Robyn climax the way she did inspired him to let go. After just a couple of minutes he was ready, and he grabbed the sides of her head just before he popped.

When Robyn felt him gripping her head she guessed he was ready and tightened the grip of her lips against his firm staff. When he did start throbbing and spurting into her mouth, Robyn felt like she was at least succeeding at this, after failing to control her own raging sex drive. Even with her poor rump aching badly, Robyn swallowed his spunk with a sense of achievement. It also made her think that what she just learned was another reason she had to follow this path. Yes, he was a cruel taskmaster, but the way he made her tingle with sexual energy was a more powerful reason to accept this as her new normal. Or abnormal, depending on how she looked at it.

Robyn had always considered herself a kind of an outsider in the real world, and now she was thinking it was maybe because she belonged in a world like this. All the kinky and demeaning things she was immersed in seemed to speak to her in ways that nothing ever did in the outside world. George somehow knew how to release the more deviant aspects of her persona. She knew that she was acting in direct opposition to everything she believed in before she met him, but now she faced the very real possibility that her life before this just hid her true nature.

Once he was done climaxing, and she was still sucking the last drops of his semen out of his softening shaft, he said, "That's a good little slut, drink my sperm. I think you know how much you love this, even though your rump is aching, you just had a pretty strong orgasm, didn't you?"

"MMMMM HMMMM!" she moaned around his cock, and it felt too damn good, so he leaned back, making it pop out of her mouth.

As soon as her mouth was free, Robyn said, "Thank you Sir. You are right, I want this even though I don't know what it is."

"It is what happens when you find your soul mate. I know what you are and what you need to feel fulfilled, and that is serving me. We share a darker nature that makes us mesh so well, why else would you accept the brutal way I am treating you?"

"I am so confused Sir, I want to be with you, but this is so hard," Robyn admitted.

"Yes it is, probably the hardest thing you have ever faced girl. It will always be the roughest right after it happens, so let's get you up and put some food in your belly. Maybe you will feel better once you eat," George said, as he began untying the ropes.

Once he got her up on her feet, he led Robyn over to a mirror so she could see her black and blue buttocks. He had her turn her back toward the mirror and look over her shoulder to see her backside, and while she did, he reached between her legs and stroked her sex. She shuddered a little when he stroked her clit, exactly the reaction he wanted.

"As bad as your bum stings, the cunt is still hot and ready for pleasure. What do you think that means Robyn?" he asked.

"That I am a freak Sir?" she asked, so utterly confused that she did not know what to think.

"Maybe, but if you are a freak, then so am I, and maybe freaks like us belong together."

"Maybe Sir, but it is all so terrifying, look at my butt! Will it ever look normal again?"

"Faster than you imagine, in a couple of days it will look like this never happened. Stop looking for excuses girl, face your fears and accept that you want and need this. You want me to bring out the sleeping tigress inside you. Face your true desires Robyn and you won't regret it."

"I am trying Sir," she said sadly.

"Let's eat, maybe you will feel better after some dinner," he said, as he escorted her to the kitchen, which smelled wonderful.

In order to get her mind off her doubts, he instructed her to remove the chicken from the oven and how to make up their plates. Then, once she placed them on the table, he decided against making her sit on her battered butt, and instead had her kneel on a cushion beside his chair. He fed both of them again, and as they ate their food, Robyn's fears receded and she decided she was not ready to quit. She was still as aroused as ever, and she decided that she would at least endure it until he had sex with her. Deep down Robyn thought that she would know what she really wanted when that time came, and she hoped he would not wait too long.

After they finished eating and Robyn cleaned up, she found him in the study again. She still had doubts she could deal with this all the time, but she was feeling much better. Her butt cheeks were still stinging, but not nearly as badly as earlier. She, like she had before, crawled to him once she reached the study. When she came up beside him, he reached out and stroked her head like you would pet a dog, and she had to admit that she felt like his puppy in training.

"Well Robyn, do you feel better about us now?" he asked in a soothing tone of voice.

"Yes Sir, thank you Sir, I do feel better, but I am still scared," she admitted.

"The question is what are you afraid of? How hard this is? Or how hot you still feel?"

"I don't know Sir, but I still want to find out," she said.

"I guessed as much. Now you will drape yourself over my lap again," he said.

She wanted to say, 'please don't hurt me again,' but all she did was thank him and assume the position. She was thoroughly surprised and delighted when he began to massage something into her battered flesh. It stung a little at first, but his touch was still electric, and after just a few minutes the pain faded. But he continued massaging her bottom and lower back, which ignited a new fire in her sex. Robyn moaned contentedly, wondering how he could pivot from cruelty to kindness so easily. But it worked, and by the time he stopped, she was totally relaxed.

"Kneel before me slave," he said, sensing he could return to reminding her of her status now that she seemed to have moved passed the crisis of confidence she expressed. As he looked down at her, once again looking up at him with a look of desire, he was pleased. He cautioned himself not to push her too hard, just enough to keep her both on edge and aroused. If he was too harsh with her early on, he risked scaring her away, and that would be a shame. Her potential was great, but he had to cultivate her more perverse desires.

In that vein, he said, "Would you like to watch a movie with me before you go home?"

"Yes Sir! Thank you Sir," Robyn exclaimed, finally something normal couples did!

He took her to his game room with the big screen TV. He took a seat at the end of a plush couch, making her lay on her side with her head in his lap. He even tossed a furry throw blanket over her lower body, and she was just thrilled. But when he started the movie, she quickly realized this was no normal movie. It was a porno flick with a man and his slave girl doing all sorts of perverted things in a dungeon.

At first it scared her, but it did not stay that way, as watching the man whipping the girl looked more sexy than cruel. She was doing the same thing George made her do, thanking him and asking for more after every stroke. Yet, even though Robyn saw the red stripes forming on her back and rump, the girl sounded far more excited than distressed. The credits said they were a real couple that liked to record their sessions, and as it went on Robyn could sense how real it was.

Since the blanket only covered her from the waist down, he spent most of the movie playing with her tits with one of his hands. He used the other one to pet her head, while he casually talked about how the dominant/submissive relationship worked because each partner played to the strength of the other. And when the movie reached the fuck scene, after a long period of painful foreplay, George moved his hand from her tits to under the blanket. His fingers found her pussy was nice and wet, which pleased him as much as the moan of pleasure she made.

Then, in the sweetest voice he ever heard, she said, "Thank you Sir."

"I know that you think you are ready to fuck me, but you are not, you are close, but I saw your resolve falter earlier today. I need to see you stick to my training regimen for at least a week without another crisis of confidence. You have always fancied yourself as a strong person, well, this lifestyle is about as hard as it gets, especially for the submissive. You have to trust that I will not break you, and I understand that you are not there yet," he said gently.

"I am asking a lot, everything actually, and that is a big ask. But, I think we both know that there is something between us, and that despite your fear, you want to explore the possibilities we can provide for each other. You would never have taken what I have done to you if you did not feel the connection with me, but it is much more than that. Our sympatico only exists because we have divergent desires that, when combined, form the ultimate Yin Yang. Do you know what I am saying girl?"

"Yes Sir, I think so. But I was never submissive until I met you," she replied, still unsure if she really was submissive.

"Maybe it was because you never met anyone that brought those feelings to the surface. Think about when I told you that you needed a spanking, how did it make you feel? Not initially mind you, but once you thought about it."

"After I thought about it?" she said, as she remembered the ride home from the restaurant. Then she replied, "It sounded kinky, but in a sexy kind of way, I guess."

"Basically, it sparked your interest, and once you went through it, I think we can both agree you reacted positively. And then the game got more intense, and still you loved it! Then today came, and it got more intense and more real, and yet you still climaxed like a shameless whore. So, tell me Robyn, do you think I could have manufactured this? Or did I just expose what you did not even know existed?"

"I am so confused Sir, but I can't walk away, I need to explore this with you."

"I know slave, and I say that because I know what you are even if you don't. And I am not even saying you are my slave, what I am saying is that you are wired for it, you just have not found your Master yet. For now, it is time to get you ready to go home, and when you get back in the morning I expect a renewed commitment from you. Seven days of service that will include at least one punishment a day, a whole lot of hard work, and a fair amount of teasing. If you prove you can handle it, you will move in on the eighth day and I will give you what you crave. Is it a deal?"

"Yes Sir, thank you Sir," Robyn replied, but she was now fixated on a new word he used. Was he planning to become her Master? If so, she liked the sound of it, knowing exactly what it meant about her newfound desires.

CHAPTER 10: SEVEN DAYS IN SALACIOUS SERVITUDE

Robyn went back to her old room after her first bruising paddling with her mind focused inward. A lot had transpired in the two days she had spent with George, and her bruised buttocks were the least of it. She barely knew him, and figuring him out was proving fruitless, yet he was so deep into her head that he knew things about her before she did. He would say things she never even considered, but once he said it, the way it resonated with her was astonishing. She had to wonder how she could not have seen it herself.

It was all happening so fast, but here she was in her bed, naked with an aching rump, except for the steel chastity belt locked to her body. As she lay in bed rubbing her hot tender cheeks and the cool hard surface of the device he attached to her, Robyn could not quell the compulsion she felt to follow this strange man. He was handsome, but his views could be considered ugly, as he made her suffer through some very difficult and demeaning activities. But, despite his cruelty, she could feel his grip on her mind and body was still intensifying.

He must have seen her tossing and turning, as her mind wrestled with all the reasons that following him both aroused and frightened her. She heard him speak to her through the earbud, as he told her, "I suspect you are struggling again, and you need your sleep slave. Remember this, if you can't handle this type of relationship you will have the chance to back out at least two more times. So just relax and take it one step at a time."

"Yes Sir," she whispered, as she wondered how he always knew what to say to calm her.

Robyn actually slept well that night, and after he roused her with the two appendages buzzing inside her pussy and rectum, she was ready to return for another day with him. She looked at, and then felt the marks still visible on her rump. Surprisingly, they did not look or feel as bad as she thought before she went to bed. He had told her that she would heal quickly, and it seemed he was right, and that helped to build her trust in him.

She washed and dressed at his direction and was back at his place in less than half an hour. Once she entered the house, she disrobed, donned her heels, and went to the kitchen where he was waiting for her to cook his breakfast. Robyn greeted him with a phrase that was spelled out in her rule book, "How may I serve you Sir?"

George proceeded to talk her through what he wanted, and she scribbled down notes once she performed each step, while waiting for the food to cook. Doing it all in the nude was still hard to accept, but she liked being naked around George. She was even getting used to wearing the high heeled shoes all the time, liking the way they made her legs look. After they ate breakfast, which had Robyn on the floor lapping up her food like a dog again, she cleaned the kitchen. Then she went upstairs to his bathroom and, under his instructions, administered her first solo enema.

It was not a pleasant experience, but it was not as bad as the first time, even without George's cock in her mouth to distract her. Once it was over and she was working on her new chore list, Robyn was oddly energized. He had given her some strange and degrading tasks, like crawling around and scrubbing the baseboards in several rooms. She even did his laundry for the first time, and she had to hand it to him, the list of instructions he left on the washer left nothing to question.

After lunch it was training time, and on day three she got her first real taste of extreme bondage. Her arms and legs were folded together and strapped to themselves, and then George situated her on her elbows and knees to crawl around more like a dog than ever. She gave him his first blowjob of the day propped up on her bound limbs. Despite the dreadfully humiliating position, she found her pussy was again tingling with an ever increasing longing. After he came, he teased her to the brink of her own orgasm, only denying her when she begged for relief. But unlike the day before, she made her plea before she reached the point of no return.

He seemed pleased with her self-control, and that made her feel good, as she slipped ever closer to accepting his absolute authority over her. It was not the way she imagined a man would seduce her, being treated so harshly seemed antithetical to falling for a guy. Yet, here she was, dreaming of the day he fully claimed her body as his. She could not fathom how she had remained so aroused for nearly three straight days, it seemed impossible. She also wondered if this was how it would feel all the time. She certainly appreciated it when he actually let her sit on a chair and eat on her own, but she also missed being hand fed. It also emphasized the fact that she was able to sit comfortably after her paddling just yesterday.

As frightening as this was in her mind, she was finding the reality was difficult, but also exhilarating. After dinner he had her shave her legs, armpits, and dispatch all of her pubic hair too. Sitting on the floor of his study, shaving her body bare, Robyn could not deny how exciting even the simple act of depilating her skin was with him watching her. Then he made her play with her pussy while telling him how badly she wanted his cock inside it. She surprised herself by how explicit and crude she was, and how much it steamed up her increasingly desperate sex. He stopped her far short of a climax, in fact, she had found that her fingers were no longer enough thanks to his more exotic methods of extracting orgasms from her. She was more excited by the fact that he was watching her masturbate.

After her little performance, he belted Robyn up, had her put on the boring track suit. Then he sent her home to study her rule book before bed. The night before she was having doubts, but after day three, her attitude definitely improved. Robyn found her second run through of her laundry list of rules and performance requirements revealed a few things she missed. This time, rather than being a daunting revelation, she started to imagine George being her Master with her as his slave. It was still a fearsome prospect, especially if she became his live in slave. But apart from sleeping in her room, she had been exactly that for three straight days.

When he told her she could stop studying and get some sleep, Robyn had the best night's rest that she had since he had erotically rocked her world the first night with him. The next six days followed a similar pattern, but with interesting variations on the basic theme. Robyn toiled, suffered, and was sexually teased to keep her simmering with desire. She slowly fell under the spell that submissives do when they find the one that makes them want to submit. The way he would inflict pain on her even had an erotic edge to it, and every punishment was followed by him taking her to the brink of ecstasy.

With her arousal constantly at the front of her mind, but not being allowed to boil over, it was becoming harder and harder to handle. But she never complained to him, she kept it to herself. She expected that once he did let her sexuality loose, she would likely explode like a stick of dynamite. As she walked to his house for the seventh time since he told her that she might be allowed to move in after a week, Robyn was hoping that she had met his expectations. The idea of moving in with him was no longer frightening, she wanted to jump his bones so badly at this point that she thought that nothing could change her mind.

George had sensed the changes in Robyn during the last few days, and even though he had ramped up the strictness of his dominance over her, she continued to follow his demands without question. He was almost ready to move her in and take her training to the next level, but today he wanted to test her resolve one last time. Before she became a resident slave in his home, Robyn needed to know what it would require. Though she learned most of it during the last week, other duties and restrictions would be added to be his live in slave. Today Robyn would learn what this kind of life actually demanded from her, and then she would have to decide if she wanted to try it.

Her arrival and first set of tasks remained constant, as she cooked his breakfast in the buff and then flushed out her bowels. Even the enemas she hated at first had become something of an erotic adventure, maybe because her butt hole was so close to her famished sex. But, either way, Robyn was finding that the things that she disliked or scared her were just becoming another part of her new and very kinky normal. Once she had completed her morning toilet, Robyn went to find George in his study, where he always waited for her.

When she got there she saw that he was standing by a window, looking out on his yard. She crawled over to him as quietly as she could, and when she reached him, she rubbed her head against his leg. It still surprised her how much she actually enjoyed being his naked slave girl, even though she still had not experienced what she expected would be the best part. She was hoping that he would tell her it was time to move in, she was ready to take that step, eager to feel his gorgeous cock inside her achingly hot sex.

"If I asked you to move in today, what would you say?" he asked, as he continued to stare out of the window.

"Yes please Sir," she said, as her arousal spiked instantly.

"That is why today we will forgo any chores, and we will spend the morning exploring the BDSM dynamic. I have a surprise for you, there is a part of the house you have not seen yet. Now put this over your head," he said, as he tossed a black velvet bag onto the floor in front of her.

Robyn put it over her head and then felt him pull the drawstring around the opening until it was snug around her neck, not tight, but it wasn't coming off either. He ordered her to stand just before he tossed her over his shoulder like a sack of potatoes. Robyn loved the way he did it, and just let herself hang there limply. She thought he took her to the front vestibule where she always stripped upon arriving. Then she heard a door open and they were moving down a stairway, she could tell by the sounds and the way he jostled her.

They reached the lower level and he walked a few steps with her on his shoulder until he put her back on her feet. "This will be our play room; I have not used it with anyone yet. But to be honest, I just brought in the basics since I found you. It will be a work in progress, much like you," he said, just before removing the hood.

Robyn looked around the large empty basement with cinderblock walls and an unfinished ceiling with exposed wooden beams. There was a corner with the water and heating equipment, and a row of round steel posts down the center. But what caught her attention were the 'basics' that he mentioned. There were several things set up around the room that made it look almost like a dungeon. An X cross, a padded sawhorse like device, a pillory, and a couple of tables that looked like they had mechanisms underneath them. Then there was the variety of paraphernalia hanging on the walls: ropes, chains, whips, and things that she had no idea what they were.

But there was a distinctive feature near the center of the room, a giant spider web made of shiny steel chains mounted between two of the steel columns. It took Robyn's breath away, as she pictured her naked body bound across it. Over the last few days, she came to enjoy being in bondage. Being his helpless plaything was a big part of her thrill, and partially her way of pretending that she had no choice. At the very least, she was at the mercy of her runaway sex drive, which ironically had not been allowed any fully satisfying results for almost a week.

Once she had a few moments to view the room, George asked, "What do you think slave?"

Feeling a flush of arousal, Robyn asked, "May I choose what you bind me to first?"

George laughed, and replied, "Yes you may, but I think I know which one already."

"If you are thinking it is the web, then you are right Sir," she said, quite provocatively.

"See? Once again we are on the same page, so your wish is granted," he said smugly.

In short order Robyn was bound to the web, but not quite in the way she envisioned, though she did not let him know that he surprised her again. She pictured being attached to it against her back, but he fixed her to it so she was facing it. Robyn found that the way it was designed left her face, breasts, and her crotch exposed through openings in the web. It was the kind of position that impressed Robyn, he was not just kinky, he was creative about it.

He stepped in front of her once she was spread eagled against the chains, and said, "You look beautiful up there, are you enjoying being caught in my web?"

"Yes Sir, very much Sir," Robyn replied seductively.

He pulled a handful of large rubber bands out of his pocket and began stretching them around the bases of her tits, making Robyn's generous mounds bloat up into firm pink balls. Then he sucked on her engorged nipples, turning the bound teen into a moaning slut whose pussy was so wet that it was leaking its juices down her thighs. Even though the tight bands squeezing into her soft breast meat made them feel like they might burst, Robyn relished the strange sensations.

Once he got his fill of sucking on her nipples, George stepped back and said, "Look at those tits of yours! They look marvelous like this! I am betting, by the look of your wet thighs, that you are enjoying the way they feel too. Am I right slave?"

"Yes Sir, I am very aroused Sir," she answered.

George reached down and fingered her juicy slit before moving that hand up to her mouth. He inserted the two fingers into her mouth, the same ones he just removed from her twat. As she greedily sucked her own wetness from his digits, Robyn moaned like she loved it, and honestly, she did. Robyn had tasted her vaginal secretions before, when she was playing with herself in her old life, but after he had made her lick up her slutty discharge several times, it now tasted so much better. No matter what he made her do, she found that she often became aroused, despite how degrading it should have felt.

"Have you ever been with another woman slave?" he asked unexpectedly.

"No Sir!" she answered emphatically, once again surprised by his surprising question.

"Don't be offended slave, you just sucked your cunt juice off my fingers. It sure sounded like you enjoyed it," he said.

"Yes Sir, but…"

"Stop making excuses! Admit how much you like how you taste!"

"Yes Sir, I do Sir," she replied, feeling chastened by his voice.

"I expect my slave to have no boundaries, to pursue what arouses her without reservations. So far you have embraced so many things that you never considered, this is just the next step."

"Yes Sir," she replied, wondering where this was leading.

"Before you decide whether to move in with me you need to know that, as I mentioned before, I am part of a community. If you become my slave you will meet some of them, either here or at the parties we host. They like to share, and that means you will have to serve other men and women to please me. No one will touch you without my approval, and whatever you do for them will really be you performing for me. Can you handle that?" he asked, seeing the shock in her eyes.

"I don't know Sir, I am just getting used to this with you, how can I imagine being with others too?" she asked, almost frantically.

"Have I been completely honest with you slave?" he asked.

"Yes Sir."

"I want you to know everything that is coming, long before it does. You will still have two chances to back out, but before you take the next step, I want you to know the broader picture. I have no intention of adding anyone else to the mix unless, or until, you beg me to let you serve another. That will only happen if you move in and experience a month of living as my slave every day. If, at that time, you cannot accept my requirements, you can still walk. Is that fair?"

"I guess so Sir, but it still frightens me," she admitted in a very meek voice.

"It should, so far everything we have done has scared you at first. But once you experienced it, the fear receded and you found how much you actually enjoyed it," he said, as he stroked her sex to remind her how aroused she was at the moment.

"Yesss Sirrr!" she cooed, as his magic fingers diverted her attention back to her excitement.

"That's better slave, follow your feelings, not your fears. I will protect you, even as I push you beyond the boundaries that hinder your full awakening. There is so much more to becoming a slave than just the sexual aspect, there is the mental trust you must have with me. Earning your trust will take time, and all I expect is that you follow my lead and see where it takes you. Can you do that Robyn?"

"I will try Sir," she said, still plagued by doubts thanks to this latest revelation. She was just getting used to him, and now he tells her that he plans on sharing her with others. And not just other men, he wanted her to be intimate with women too! She had to wonder what other surprises he had in store for her, but she also had to admit that he planted the seeds in her head before he did anything. But this new disclosure seemed much more daunting, however, so far, everything he revealed was scarier in her head than it actually was in reality.

"One day you will understand why I am doing this, but for now, no more talk, it is time to play," he said, as he started to move behind her.

He casually moved her hair over the front of her shoulders to expose all the freckled flesh of her shoulders, an area that had yet to feel a lash. Over the last few days, he had introduced her to all sorts of painfully erotic games, but after her harsh bum paddling, he had refrained from impact play. He had given her a taste of hot wax, ice cubes, clamps, suction devices, and a few other types of uncomfortable sensation games, but now it was time for her first erotic whipping.

He had picked a supple multi-strand flogger that would sting, but not cause any lingering bruising. Her bum had already healed from the spanking earlier in the week. She had come to realize that as bad as it felt, like he promised, it left no lingering marks and her skin recovered completely. Now, he was going to give her a taste of the leather, but he would make sure that while she felt that distinctive burn, he would keep her other fire stoked too.

"I am going to lash your back slave, and it will hurt, but just like your ass paddling, I promise it will feel worse than it is. Do you trust me slave?" he asked, as he worked the tangles out of the whip before he started on her.

"Yes Sir," she replied, as she tried to brace herself for another painful experience.

"Good girl, " he said, just before delivering two quick lashes across her shoulders.

"AAAHHH! Thank you Sir! May I have another?" Robyn cried out.

He did not answer her, he just continued, giving her four more twin lashes between her replies to each pair. But then he stepped up to her, turned the handle around, and rubbed it against her sex. It prompted Robyn to start moaning again. Once he had her nicely worked up, he moved back, and gripping the damp whip handle properly, he gave her another set of five double lashes. Her vocal responses were much more animated after he worked up her cunt. When that set was over, he used the whip handle to stoke her up again.

But this time, while he 'handled' her sex, he whispered in her ear, "Admit how much you really love being treated like this slave."

"Yesss Sirr, I love thissss" she purred, unable to deny how aroused she felt.

"Good girl," he said, just before he stopped teasing her and began another round of lashing her freshly striped back. By the end of the third round, he had turned her back into a nice pink hue, with slightly darker stripes showing where the whip had landed. When he finished the third round and stepped back up to tease her twat, he used his hand instead of the whip.

"Oh my! What a juicy cunt you have slave, does my whip arouse you?"

"Yesss Sirrr," she answered, though she knew it was the combined effect of the whip and the way he was teasing her sex. By now she had come to expect the teasing, and the fact that he never let her climax. But today was a little different, as Robyn knew this was her final test before he decided to move her in and give her all that he had denied her so far. She did trust that he would deliver what she craved, and after a week of continually unrequited arousal, she was pretty sure that it would be an amazing experience.

"Good slave," he said, as he toyed with her twitching twat.

"Thank you Sirrr," she cooed contentedly.

He continued to whip and toy with her a half dozen more times, and as the whip marks got darker and angrier, her voice began to fade. But her sex remained animated and responsive every time he teased it. George was thrilled that her pain tolerance was growing thanks to the fact that he kept her aroused throughout her most of her training. She was clearly in a fog when he stopped and he carefully removed her from the web. She literally fell into his arms and whimpered because it hurt when her back landed against his chest.

He helped her to stand and walked her over to the device that looked like a big sawhorse, making her lie face down over the padded upper rail. It was only six inches wide and her body extended beyond each side, but it also pushed her rubber band bound boobs apart, while bisecting her cleavage. He strapped her upper thighs to the angled legs and it made her rump stick out provocatively behind the bench. He came around to the front and attached her wrists to the bottoms of the front legs, so she had to keep her palms on the floor to steady herself.

He stepped in front of her and lifted her head up by grabbing her hair, and he said, "Suck my cock slave," as he pulled his staff from his pants and slapped her cheeks with it.

Robyn was in pain, her back certainly ached almost as bad as her rump had a few days earlier, but she was also far more aroused than she was back then. Seeing his cock in front of her face triggered the reaction ingrained in her mind after sucking it at least three times a day over the last week. As much as she wanted to feel it inside her sex, she had to admit that feeling it inside her mouth was something she truly enjoyed. She even liked it when he called her his cocksucker, kind of like how every demeaning thing he said almost felt like compliments. He wanted a sex crazed slut for a slave and Robyn was beginning to feel like one. Now she viewed his derogatory comments in a whole new way, one that utterly defied logic.

But this was never about logic or reason, everything he wanted was the epitome of depraved behavior. And though she cautiously stepped into it at first, it was becoming like a runaway freight train. Every day with him was nourishing her newly exposed deviant desires, the games they were playing were changing her in ways that astonished her. And this denial thing, this week of yearning without any real relief, was pushing her even deeper under his spell. He knew how to get her hot, and keep her that way. It was making her desperate to succeed and earn the kind of sexual ecstasy she experienced the first night with him. Deep down she dreamed it would be even better!

Once Robyn was diligently sucking his shaft, George reached down and applied a lotion to Robyn's stippled back. It stung her at first, and she moaned sadly, but never relented from her duty to please his cock with her mouth. He was satisfied with her behavior and it made it easy to take the next step, to show this virginal slave what she could really expect from him. Once he gave her another belly full of spunk, it would be almost time to make her his offer. As Robyn happily slurped down his load, George began thinking about shagging this little slut. She was not the only one that wanted to end the extended tease, but at least he had plenty of blowjobs this week to keep him from taking her too soon. It would also make her first shag last a lot longer, as his stamina was also at its peak with all the attention she gave his dick this last week.

CHAPTER 11: MAKING HIS MOVE

After he filled her belly with his semen again, he spent quite a while teasing her to the brink. He took a seat behind her bent over body and worked her sex until she screamed for release, only to sit back and let her come back down from her high. After six trips to the edge of ecstasy, Robyn was weeping, as the latest tease had left her frantic for relief. She thought she would go mad if this continued much longer. But then, when she expected another round of torturously scarce pleasure, he had a huge surprise for her.

As she was wallowing in her misery, he stood up and pulled his cock from his pants. Even though he climaxed not too long ago, watching how she reacted to his incessant teasing had given him another erection. What he planned would be the cruelest thing he could do to her in this instant, but he also knew it would all but insure she accepted the offer he would make her today. He stepped up behind her and carefully aimed his shaft at her twitching twat hole. Without warning, he slid it all the way up into her saturated snatch.

When his hips soundly met her rump, it dawned on her what he just did, and she screamed, "Thank you SIR!"

But just as quickly, he pulled it out and walked around to face her again. He could see the look of disappointment in her eyes, but her initial vocal reaction spoke louder about the effect it actually had on her. This was a critical moment, he just gave her a fleeting taste of what was coming, and now he had to give her mind the reason to come back for more. The way her twat clutched at his shaft when he was inside her told him how well she would respond to a nice long fuck. But before he would grant her that wish, she would have to agree to another set of rules.

So, for now, another exercise in bonding was on the menu, when he said, "How did that feel slave?"

"Wonderful Sir!" she replied hopefully.

"Look at how wet my cock is slave, now clean it up!" he said forcefully.

"Yes Sir, thank you Sir," she replied, and then she opened her mouth so he could slide it in, and he did. She suckled it lovingly, liking the way her pussy juices tasted on his hot staff.

While she sucked, he said, "You have come a long way in the last week slave. Do you think you are ready to move in with me?"

"MMMMM HMMMM," she moaned passionately around the dick inside her mouth.

"There will be more rules and it will not be an easy transition, since my expectations will be much more demanding. Once my cock is clean, I will release you and let you read the rules for a slave in residence, and once you do, I will ask you the question again."

She moaned her acknowledgment again, still mainly focused on the hard shaft inside her mouth. Robyn had expected more rules, he liked rules and making her follow them. At first, they seemed so daunting, but as she grew accustomed to them, she found they helped her embrace her role. 'How else can you become a slave if you don't

148

act like one?' He was fond of asking her that question, and she was beginning to understand what he meant.

Once he was satisfied with her oral attention, but not bothering to climax again, he released her from the bench. It was lunch time, and he had worked up a hunger. Sadly, for Robyn the food she ate did nothing to satisfy the other hunger she felt, but she hoped her relief was getting closer. After they ate he had her kneel on the floor in the study, where she read the additional rules that she would have to follow when she moved into his house. It was very strict and demanding, but the only part that discouraged her was the sleeping arrangements. Rather than sleeping with him, he would keep two cages in his room for her nightly repose. One of them would be comfortable, for when she performed well, and the other would be used as a punishment, if she did not.

Once again, it was a lot to digest, as he made it clear that she could only do what he wanted, and she had to surrender any and all choice in her life. He did note that, once he broke her cherries, both vaginal and anal, his voracious sexual appetite would require their frequent use. That, of course, was what Robyn wanted to hear. And despite the anal aspect that he abruptly introduced; she was not at all surprised. And though it was scary to think about, since that was how it always was, Robyn was getting used to trying just about anything.

When she was done she closed the folder and looked up at George, and he asked her, "Well slave, are you up for another, and much tougher challenge? Are you ready to become my live in slave girl?"

"Yes Sir, if it pleases you Sir," she replied, and he appreciated how quickly she took to the etiquette of submissive speech. He had admonished her often in the last week, making her speak clearly, but also demurely. She had already learned to reply so that she deferred to his desires, even as she expressed her own.

"How would you inform your parents' servants if you were taking a vacation away from home?" he asked.

"I guess I would send them a text," she said.

"I figured as much," he said, as he pulled her cell phone out of his pocket. He handed it to her and said, "Type the message and show it to me first."

Robyn typed, 'Hey old folks! Some friends invited me to their beach house for a few weeks, and I am leaving tomorrow.' Then she handed the phone to him.

He looked at it and asked, "Old folks?"

"That is what I always call them, I know it is mean, but that was who I was," she admitted.

"And you don't want to make them think anything has changed, I suppose that is prudent. No need to reveal your new demeanor and make them wonder what has changed," he said, as he started typing on her phone.

When he was done, George handed it back to Robyn and watched her eyes go wide. He had changed tomorrow to tonight, and added a line that Robyn would come home to pack a bag before she left today. She looked up at him after she read it and smiled brightly, as she realized that her goal to jump his bones was even closer than she hoped.

He said, "Yes slave, you will make one more trip home after dinner. And yes, when you get back you are going to get what a horny slut like you craves."

"Yes Sir! Thank you Sir!" she exclaimed enthusiastically.

"You may send it now," he said, and she did.

Before they could do anything else a text chimed on the phone, as Rose replied, 'That is nice dear, have a good time!' Robyn showed George the reply, and he said, "Very good, now we can go over the new rules."

That started a long discussion with Robyn, where George grilled her on the basic rules first. Once he was satisfied that she understood the first set of rules, he began to discuss the new set of guidelines for living with him. Though his world was full of rules and practices she would have to follow, Robyn was so intent on jumping George that she just absorbed his comments. She did not even bother questioning her less than ideal sleeping arrangements.

He clarified his intentions regarding her cages, once he took her down to the basement where they were waiting under a cover in the corner. She had not noticed them before, but once he pulled the cover off and she saw them, she wondered which one was the 'comfortable' one. There was a small square cage that looked like a dog crate, and she guessed that if she curled up inside it that it might be bearable. The other was leaning against the wall, a tall narrow cage that looked a little like a coffin made of bars.

He said, "The small cage will have a padded dog cushion on the bottom, and will be quite comfortable.

This is the standing cage, and yes it will be set up in my room fully erect. If you are a bad slave, then you will sleep standing up, a position that will make sure you learn whatever lesson you need to. Is that perfectly clear slave?"

"Yes Sir," she answered sheepishly, not really liking either option.

"That is not to say that you will always sleep in these cages. If you perform exceptionally, I will grant you nights in bed with me," he said, dangling another carrot for her to follow.

"Yes Sir, thank you Sir," she replied in a more upbeat tone.

"Now help me get these up to my room," he said.

They took the tall one up first, and though it was not very heavy, it was awkward and was more of a workout for Robyn than George. When he stood it up in a corner of his room, Robyn looked at it fearfully, not wanting to try to sleep while forced to stand inside it all night. The second trip brought the 'comfy' cage up to his room, and when he placed it beside his bed, Robyn liked the location he picked. At least she would be closer to him right next to his bed, but she still did not know why he wanted to cage her at night. But she remembered that she had agreed to live here as his slave, and these cages were a tangible reminder of the reality of that choice.

He pulled a large pet cushion from under his bed, and handed it to her, as he said, "Put it in the cage by the bed, and then crawl into it to give it a try."

"Yes Sir, thank you Sir," Robyn replied, as she took the cushion.

She got down on her knees and opened the latch and door to the cage, and then she slipped the pad into it, finding that it fully covered the bottom. When she crawled inside she kind of liked the feeling, like she was his pet, a rather comforting feeling. The more submissive she acted, the more she felt it was right for her, no matter what her common sense tried to tell her. Once she crawled inside she found that if she drew her knees up toward her chest and was lying on her side, it was rather relaxing.

"Do you like it slave?" George asked, after watching her find a way to lie down inside it.

"Yes Sir, thank you Sir, it is kind of cozy," she said. But internally, she wondered what it would feel like in the morning after a night balled up inside the cage.

"You can get out now, and then take a turn in the other cage," he said.

"Yes Sir, thank you Sir," she replied.

Robyn crawled out of the short cage and over to the tall one before she stood up and opened the door. George told her to back into it, which she did, finding that it was so narrow that her arms were trapped by her sides and pressing against the bars. She watched him step forward and close the door, also learning that it squeezed against her front and back sides too. But whoever designed it had installed circular openings in the door that left her tits sticking out the front of it. The way he was smiling at her once he had latched the door closed made Robyn nervous.

"I have a couple of things to do before I send you on your last trip across the street, and I think spending some time in this cage will be good for you. It should instill in you a strong desire to behave well to avoid long nights inside it," George said.

"Yes Sir, thank you Sir," she replied, not thrilled by his pronouncement, but aware that her agreement with him left all decisions up to him.

Robyn spent several hours waiting for George to come back, and he was right, she learned that standing in the narrow cage for so long was a strong deterrent for her to avoid bad behavior. The only movement she could manage was shifting her weight from one foot to the other, and while she waited, she pondered her desire to enter into this kind of life. The last week was the most exciting of her life, but it was also the most scary and confusing. How could she justify being his pet, his sex toy, or worse, his whipping girl?

The truth was that she did not know, everything she was doing to pursue this strange type of relationship was nothing like her old self would have tolerated. The key was George, because, for reasons she did not understand, it was like she was mesmerized by him and she could deny him nothing. It defied logic, but this was a matter of the heart, and she had secretly hoped she could find a man who understood her. What Robyn never expected was meeting someone who could see things about her that she had failed to recognize on her own.

The clues were there, she had been fascinated by porn movies that showed young girls being manhandled by older men. She had not been dreaming of a loving and gentle relationship; her nascent sexuality was aroused by the rougher side of intimacy. But it was when George first told her that she deserved a spanking that she had to seriously confront her hidden desires. It was a fact that the idea of being spanked by George got her all hot and bothered, and it became the catalyst that sent her on this perverted journey.

He had spent her first week making her perform like a pet monkey, while denying her the sexual relief that his teasing kept simmering. This only reinforced her budding need to explore the rough sex she had dreamed about even before she met George. She tried to tell herself that once she experienced it, she would know for sure, but she also wondered if she would just become an addict. The way he made her climax that first night was still bright in her memory, and she knew that it had the potential to override her common sense. Not that she had much of that left after the last week of naked servitude.

Robyn tried to remind herself that even though she had agreed to move in with George, it was just another trial period. After a month she would get to decide if she wanted to continue or end it. However, she also worried that a month of the kind of explosive sexual satisfaction she was now anticipating might cloud her ability to make a rational decision. Then again, there were not many choices she made since meeting George that would be considered normal. He was totally clear about what he wanted, and so far, she had done whatever he demanded. Granted, all of it was fueled by her intense desire to jump his bones.

But even though that was what kept driving her forward, the things he did to her did nothing to lessen her commitment. The kinkier he got, the harsher he got, none of it mattered, because all of it stoked an internal fire that was ignited just a week ago. The night he tied her to the bed and made her climax until she passed out from sexual overload was seared into her psyche. There was no way she could walk away until she learned what it would be like once she experienced actual sexual intercourse with George. But that also worried her, because if it was as good, or better, than she imagined, she doubted she could ever walk away from it. She also worried that after a full month of such a sexualized existence that she would be so dependent on those feelings that she would be unable to live without it. She was beginning to understand the full weight of this game, and once he took her virginity, she suspected that she could become an incurably addicted slut. Not that the prospect seemed all that bad when she remembered what he did to her a week ago.

By the time George returned to release her, Robyn was still determined to proceed, but she had not resolved all her misgivings. She wondered if she ever would, but that was another aspect to her relationship with George, the unknown. He had revealed things to her, and about her, that were changing her view of herself in dramatic ways. She had to accept that such a huge change in her mindset would also create a lot of doubt. So far, every fear she faced turned out to be far less daunting in reality than it was in her head. But now she was facing a long term change, one that might change her completely, and forever!

With that in mind, she meekly followed him to the kitchen and, for the first time, cooked his dinner by herself while he watched her. She would look to him often during the meal prep, and he just smiled at her,

156

which was enough approval to keep her happy. They shared their meal like a vanilla couple, as he actually allowed her to eat with silverware while sitting across from him at the table. He informed her that her trip home would be short, just long enough for her to pack a bag and then return.

After their dinner, and her mandatory kitchen clean up, Robyn headed to the study where he was waiting for her. When she saw him with the chastity belt sitting on the ottoman in front of his chair, she wondered why he would make her wear it for just a short trip to her parents' home and back. As usual, she crawled over to him and knelt beside his chair to await his orders. She saw that another boring sweat suit was folded underneath the chastity belt with a pair of sneakers on the floor next to it.

"As you can see, you will wear the chastity belt for your last errand. You will understand why once you get dressed and are on your way, now put it on," he said.

"Yes Sir," she said, as she stood up and picked up the device.

It was the first time he told her to put it on by herself, as he seemed to enjoy installing it on her body. But she knew the procedure by now, and wrapped the waistband around her body and matched the slot with the D-ring to hold it together. It was the crotch piece that worried her, but he had changed the interior appendages to rubber inserts, and the anal one was lubricated. It was actually easy to insert both of them, as her sex was as slick as ever. Once she aligned the end of the crotch band to the waist belt, he handed her the padlock, and she locked herself into it.

Robyn donned the track suit and sneakers next, and once she stood up again, he did too. He took the zipper handle, positioned just below her tits as usual, and lowered it until he reached her belly button. This made her nervous, because the sides of the jacket barely contained her tits now, and she wondered if they might pop out when she started walking. She was about to learn that would be the least of the challenges she was about to face.

CHAPTER 12: A ROUGH ROAD TO ECSTASY

When they reached the front door, Robyn realized that if she walked slowly and carefully, her breasts remained relatively secure inside the jacket. George put the bud in her ear and tested it before opening the door. She looked at him while thinking that once she returned from this short excursion her real training as a sex slave would begin, the operative word that made it exciting being 'sex.' She could not remember anything she wanted more than wanting him to ravage her and turn her into his actual sex slave.

"Before you go, I have added a little twist to your trip this time," George said, as he pulled a small remote control out of his pocket. He pressed a button and Robyn felt both of the shafts impaling her start buzzing, mildly, but they definitely inflamed her arousal. George saw her start to tremble once the dildos were activated, and he smiled at her knowingly.

"There are four settings and right now you are feeling the lowest one. I will bump it up one level after five minutes, and again five minutes later. I suspect the fourth level will push you very hard, so it would be in your best interest to get back in less than fifteen minutes, before I turn it to the fourth setting. Are you ready to go?"

Gritting her teeth, as she tried to resist the arousal that was already building up inside her, she said, "Yes Sir, thank you Sir."

"Then off you go, " he said, as he gestured with his arm to usher her out the door.

As Robyn began her trek to complete her last excursion to her parents' house, she quickly realized what he had done. By lowering the jacket zipper, he impeded her ability to move too quickly or risk exposing her tits. With this new game, she realized how much she enjoyed these perverted twists to normally bland events. Just a little trip across the street to provide the illusion she was going away was turned into a perverse sexual game. She estimated that she could do it, five minutes to get to her room, five more to pack clothes she would not wear, and then five to get back to his place.

When she reached the house another worry beset her, as she hoped to avoid seeing anyone while she was in there. Robyn doubted she could speak clearly with her sex twitching around the vibrators assailing both of her nether holes. Luckily, as she quietly entered, she heard voices from the direction of the kitchen, which left her a clear path to the stairs and her room. She made it to her destination, but as soon as she got inside and closed the door, she doubled over when he upped the vibrators to the next setting.

As she was struggling to get a grip on herself and pushing back the climax that almost caught her off guard, she rushed to pack a bag and get out of the house before he increased it again. She respected how well he could play her, always finding ways to make her push her limits to the edge. Once the bag was packed, rather messily because of her need for speed, she made her way back to the front door. But just a few steps away from it, George kicked her into another gear.

The sudden onslaught of vibrations tearing through her loins made her stop and brace herself against a wall to push back her urge to climax. It only took a few moments, but with the Rose and Albert just in the other room, the hardest part was keeping quiet. She wanted to scream, or at least moan, but she held her voice in check and wobbled to the front door before slipping out of it as quietly as she could.

Once Robyn was outside, she had to brace herself against the door for a few moments, as she found that even walking a few steps at this setting was incredibly arousing. She looked across the street and the relatively short distance she had to traverse now seemed like it was a million miles away. She wondered how she could make it without exploding into an orgasm. But she had to do it, though she knew it would be nearly impossible, but she was still determined to succeed.

Once she caught her breath, Robyn began a steady and methodical walk toward George's place. By the time she reached the street she had found a gait that kept her from popping her cork, but halfway across George upped it to the fourth setting. It hit her like train, and as she stumbled with nothing to grab to steady herself, Robyn had to force herself to keep walking. When she reached his driveway, she had to stop for a moment, she was so damn close that she had to blot out all distractions to suppress the climax that threatened to overwhelm her.

She knew it was a losing battle and she looked at the front door of his house, not more than a hundred feet away, but she was scared to move. Then she heard his voice, "Are you having some trouble slave?"

"Please Sir, please turn them down! If I move I might just explode!" she replied, sounding frantic.

"I see, well I might be willing to grant your wish. But, if I do, there will be a price to pay. Are you willing to take that risk?" he asked her mockingly.

"Yes Sir, please turn them off Sir!" she replied, even more desperately.

"Now it's off you want? Make up your mind slave!"

"No Sir! Yes Sir! Just do whatever you think is best Sir!"

"How's this?" he said, as he dialed it back to the first setting.

"Aaaahhh! Thank you Sir! That's much better," she replied, but she was still dangerously close to losing it.

"Here is the deal slave, you have ten seconds to reach the front door before I turn it all the way up again. On my mark, ready...set...GO!" he snapped.

Robyn just reacted, doing her best to drag her wheeled suitcase behind her, as she sprinted to the door. As she ran, the need to move swiftly kept her focus off of the twin intruders still rattling madly around inside her. But there was no way she could not have noticed how her tits popped out of her jacket and flopped about during her run. Even though it was humiliating, she kind of enjoyed knowing that only one man was witnessing her demeaning sprint.

Just a few feet away from the door he did exactly what he warned, and this time it sent her to the ground, landing hard on her hands and knees. But then, just as suddenly, it stopped. It still left her fighting back another near orgasm that threatened to overwhelm her. While she was trying to calm herself down, the door opened and George grabbed her by her hair. He pulled her into the house, and she barely managed to avoid being dragged, as she scrambled inside the door. The abrupt way he did it actually helped her quell the urge to climax, again resisting the irresistible.

"You have learned how to control your urges quite well slave. You have not climaxed yet, have you?" he asked, but he knew.

"No Sir," she whimpered with her desperation for sexual relief now peaking.

"Then maybe it is time to let the slut free, what do you think?" he asked, knowing she was primed and ready for him to fully enjoy.

"I hope so Sir, but that is up to you," she replied breathlessly, even though she just wanted to scream, 'DAMNIT! PLEASE FUCK ME!'

In that moment she realized that this trip was designed to work her up into a sexual frenzy, and as she trembled on her hands and knees, Robyn knew he succeeded. In all her life she never wanted anything more than she wanted to let her inner slut out to release the pent up sexual tension that he just pushed to the breaking point. She was afraid to move with her sex still clutching at the dormant shaft nestled inside it. Afraid that any movement might spike it back towards a climax she doubted she could continue to resist any longer.

George watched her there on the floor, still twitching slightly from the consequences of her little trip. She had lost her grip on her suitcase, so while she regained her composure one last time, he retrieved it and closed the door. He waited until she appeared to become calm and the twitching subsided. He did notice that the inner thighs of her pants were soaked, and that made him smile.

"Up on your feet slave!" George suddenly snapped.

He smiled again when she immediately responded, but oh so slowly, seeing how she was afraid to arouse herself again. When she reached her feet, Robyn looked at him and he saw the sheer desperation in her eyes. He reached forward and unzipped her jacket before pulling it off her. Then he reached to her waist and yanked her pants down, and after ordering her to step out of them and kick off her sneakers, he handed her the key to the padlock.

"Remove the belt slave," he said.

"Yesss Sirrr," she purred, feeling she was on the brink of the sexual escapade she had been dreaming about all week. She knew that whatever she had imagined, he would twist it up and deliver it in a way that she would never see coming. It was like he had read her mind when, after the belt was lying on the floor and she was naked again, he blindfolded her. As he strapped it in place behind her head, she welcomed it, wanting nothing to distract her from the sensations she was sure were about to explode from deep within her.

"I am taking you down to our playroom, I have a surprise for you there," he said, as he placed his hands on her shoulders from behind and began steering her in the right direction.

164

"Yes Sir! Thank you SIR!" she replied loudly and lustily.

Robyn loved the way his hands felt on her shoulders and blindly walked where he steered her. When they reached the stairs to the basement, he told her to step down, and she carefully took each step down into his dungeon. When they reached the floor, he maneuvered her to the place where he planned to bind her. Knowing how much pent up sexual energy was simmering inside Robyn, he decided that restraining her for the first part of this evening's festivities was prudent.

They came upon a rectangular table and he made her climb up on it and lay down on her belly. He started with her arms, folding them together over her lower back before wrapping them in rope from her wrists to her elbows, fusing her lower arms to each other. The next part was a bit trickier, as he wound multiple strands of rope around her upper body and getting them under her body needed some maneuvering. Once he was done, Robyn had a half dozen strands of rope above and another six below her tits, which he tightly cinched behind her back. He tied another rope to the ones binding her upper arms and chest to a steel ring a hanging a couple of feet above her back.

He moved to her legs next, which were lying flat against the table with just her feet hanging over the edge of it. He folded her left leg up against her thigh and wound another dozen windings of rope around her leg, tightening the ropes so much that her heel was digging into her rump cheek. He did the same to her right leg and then tied a rope to each of her ankles. The other ends of those two ropes were pulled up and secured to the steel ring above her back. The next thing he added was a wide leather belt that he slid under her belly before buckling it together just above the crack of her rump. One last rope was attached to the belt and the ring directly above it.

George inspected the bindings to make sure they were all secure and would not loosen under stress. Then he activated the winch that the ring was hanging from and lifted Robyn up a few inches above the table. He stopped it and moved the table away before returning and lowering her a little, so she was at the right level for his design. She had been quiet throughout the process, but once she was suspended her low moans indicated that she was feeling the strain of her position.

"How do you feel slave?' he asked, as he spun her around to face him.

"Helplessly horny Sir," she replied, making him chuckle.

"That's the way a slave should feel," he said, as he began gathering her hair behind her head while winding a rope into it. Once her hair was securely knotted, he tossed the end of the rope through the suspension ropes so it was resting between her buttocks. Then he walked away for a moment and came back to show her a shiny metal tube that was bent into the shape of a question mark. The bottom had a hollow ring mounted to it and the curved end had a shiny looking ball attached to it.

"This is an anal hook, now suck on the ball to get it nice and wet," he said, as he moved the curved end up to her lips.

Robyn sucked on the ball, making sure to get as much saliva on it now that she knew where it was going.

It started to sink in that her first foray into sexual intercourse would be while she was stringently bound, suspended, and likely with a hook up her ass. Robyn realized that he would never do anything with her that could be remotely considered normal. She had imagined being entwined with his body the first time, but as she sucked on the ball that was about to take its place inside her butt hole, she accepted that his kinks were baked into this relationship.

Robyn could not deny she was aroused, and when he did install the hook in her asshole, her sex trembled with desire. Then he tied the other end to the rope wound into her hair and cinched it tight enough that she had to pull her head back and face forward. The way it was tugging against her tail bone only added to her frustrating arousal, as she could feel her pussy was twitching madly.

Once he was done, George stripped and then spun her around again, this time with his erection pointing at her face. He saw her eyes fixated on his cock, smiling when she licked her lips sexily. He knew she was ripe and ready to be fucked, but first he wanted to hear her beg for it.

"If you want me to pop your cherry, virgin slave, then you better beg for it like a hot slut."

"Yes Sir! Thank you Sir! Please Sir, please fuck me like a cheap slut! I am aching to feel you inside my hot wet cunt! I want to become your sex slave! It is all I can think and dream about Sir! I need to feel you take me and make me into a mindless fuck toy, I want to grovel at your feet and do whatever you command! Please Sir! Please grant me the honor of getting fucked by you!" Robyn cried out desperately.

George replied, "Just a week of training and look how far you have…come! Now suck on this to get it ready to ravage that slutty cunt of yours!" as he pushed his staff between her lips.

Robyn had no time to reply, but her enthusiastic mouth spoke volumes, as she devoured the dick she desperately wanted inside her sex. But she was so close, and she was happy to prime his staff for the moment she wanted so badly. She could not believe that she was this close to her goals, both getting screwed and experiencing the orgasms she expected it would give her. After almost a week without sexual satisfaction, coupled with the way he kept her aroused, and often pushed to the brink of ecstasy, she needed relief. And at this point, she did not care that he planned to take her virginity while she was hanging from the ceiling like a side of beef.

When he was satisfied that she was giving him her best blowjob yet, he pushed her back and his cock sprang free. Then he spun her around again and grabbed her by her ankles, as he aimed his cock at her winking cunt. It looked juicy and inviting, and though he had teased her all week long, he also denied himself the pleasure of plunging his cock into her snatch. Looking at her hanging there in front of him, he was ready to take her to the next level.

Once he had her steadied, he moved his right hand up her back and he grabbed her bound lower arms. Then he used his left to guide the head of his cock into Robyn's eager snatch, and the bulbous end easily slid into her soaking wet hole. The way she trembled and cooed when his dick breached the outer folds of her vulva made

George's dick throb with anticipation. But before taking the final plunge, he moved his left hand up beside the right one, so he could attain maximum thrust.

"Are you ready to become my sex slave Robyn?" he asked sternly.

"YES SIR! PLEASE SIR!" she cried out, just before he yanked hard on her arms and thrust his hips forward. His cock drilled deep into her snatch so fast that she barely felt it until his hips slammed into her crotch.

"THANK YOU SIR! OH FUCK! THAT FEELS SO GOOD!" Robyn screamed at the top of her lungs.

Then he started thrusting, mainly using his arms to push her suspended body back forth while adding extra thrusts from his hips. Her screams of pleasure rang through the large room, as he fucked her hard and fast, thrilled by how saturated her cunt felt. It was so wet, yet so tight too, as he felt her internal muscles pulsating against his pounding staff. He was not moving too fast, being more intent on slamming his body roughly against her crotch.

Robyn was experiencing a kind of bliss she never thought was possible, and it was building in intensity as her sex was spiraling towards an immense orgasm. She was grunting and groaning from every thrust, loving the way he was slamming into her. There was nothing gentle about his approach, he was screwing her the way she wanted, the way those videos she watched looked like. But with her arousal finally on a crash course that she could not avoid, Robyn knew she had to find her voice.

Using all her willpower, she howled, "PLEASE SIR! PLEASE LET ME COME!"

"Come for me my slutty little slave," he said seductively.

Since his voice already had an excessive influence on her, his command put her over the top. Her first orgasm in almost a week hit her hard and she cried out her thanks just before she erupted. However, when the climax hit her this time, her cunt opened up like a flood gate. She barely noticed how much juice her cunt spewed all over them, but George did, and that inspired him to pound her even harder and faster.

Robyn's head was spinning, the first orgasm was spectacular, far better than her first encounter with George. She was bound in a much more stressful position, and his cock was deep inside her inexperienced sex, and both factors added to how exciting the loss of her virginity was for the increasingly perverted girl. Then, right after her first orgasm started, he became even more aggressive, which sent her hurtling into another one.

"OH FUCK! OH SHIT! I'M COMING AGAIN SIR!" She screamed in distress, as it hit her so fast that she could not seek his permission first.

"Come all you like my sweet little whore," he said, and she could hear how pleased he sounded, and it gave her the green light to really let herself go. But it was not like she had any control left once she started climaxing.

He fucked her to at least two more orgasms, but to her it was like one long continuous one. And when he was satisfied that her sexual hunger was sufficiently quenched, he withdrew and spun her around again. The way she sucked his cock this time was a sight to see, even though she was in a serious orgasmic fog. But her instincts took over and she attacked his cock like her life depended on it. She could taste her cunt on his staff and it made her heart flutter, he had finally taken her virginity and made her his slutty sex slave!

Any doubts about whether what she endured was worth it were dispelled by the amazing feelings coursing through her body. As good as she had hoped it would feel was far exceeded and, once again, reality with George was far better than what she imagined. In this moment Robyn felt her compulsion to follow this man growing exponentially, and her reservations about becoming a sex slave were consumed by the flames of her incredibly intense passion.

George had almost come inside her, not that it would have mattered since she was on the pill, but he wanted her to suck his cunt drenched dick and swallow his spunk after their first tryst. Since he planned on fucking her again later, he wanted his first load to go down her throat. It would help his next foray into her tight twat last much longer. His stamina was built up with all the oral she gave him this last week, but he planned on an extended sexual marathon once he finished here.

Noting how she just displayed a new talent, he wanted to investigate it further before releasing her and taking her up to his room. Once she slurped down another dose of his sperm, and then licked his cock clean, he moved behind her again. He looked at her bright pink twat, noting how infused with blood and swollen it was. It was also as wet as ever, and when he speared it with his index finger, her body shuddered and it clutched at his digit.

"Do you realize that there is a puddle on the floor that came out of your cunt?" he asked.

"I'm sorry Sir, I could not control myself, forgive me if I peed on you," she replied, now fearful that she lost control of her bladder when she was coming.

"Did my cock taste like piss when you just sucked it?"

"No Sir, it tasted like...my cunt?" she replied, suddenly feeling confused.

"What you experienced my naïve little slave is called female ejaculation, and I am going to see if you can do it again," he said in a jovial tone.

"Yes Sir...AAAAH! AAAAH! AAAAH!" Robyn yelped, unable to finish thanking him before he distracted her.

George plunged his index and middle fingers all the way into her sex, and he began to rub the tips of them against her vaginal wall just behind her clit. It gave her a sensation she never expected, it almost felt like he was rubbing her clit. She had no idea that he was manipulating her G-spot. Her immediate reaction gave him the provocation to begin finger banging her, hard and fast. He had to grab her left ankle with his free hand to steady her when she began bucking in her bondage. He knew she would pop soon, as he slammed his fingers into her sex. He had balled up his thumb and free fingers, so it was almost like he was punching her twat.

Robyn's head was spinning from the brutal assault on her sex, it was painful, but it was also driving her toward another orgasm. A strange pressure was building up inside her, almost like an urge to pee, but not exactly. She instinctually knew that when this new sensation came to fruition that she would be launched into another mind blowing climax. She could feel her sex clutching at the fingers raking against that spot inside it. She was hurtling toward another new kind of sexual experience, as if losing her virginity was not enough.

George could feel her sex twitching and flexing against his fingers, knowing she was getting close to climaxing again. Even though she was stringently bound, being suspended left her some room to wiggle, and that was what she was doing with a vengeance. Her whole body was reacting to her oncoming orgasm and he enjoyed her instinctual struggling to escape the intensity that was rapidly building to a boiling point.

Then she made an impassioned plea, "PLEASE LET THIS SLUT COME SIR!" sounding absolutely frantic.

"Come for me slut!" he barked, while yanking his fingers out of her snatch.

"THANK YOU SIR!" Robyn roared, as she began bucking wildly.

George was presented with a sight that impressed him, when her orgasm caused both her cunt and asshole to prolapse. Seeing the bright pink inner flesh blossoming from her tight little anus was utterly unexpected, but then something much better happened. Her twat began to expel a powerful jet of girl come, winking in a way that looked like it was pumping the fluid out. He was ready for this possibility, and managed to capture most of it in small metal pail.

Robyn was lost in ecstasy; it was almost like an out of body experience. She knew she was struggling and bouncing about, but she was not controlling her gyrations. And she was right about this new sensation, it was almost like she was pissing fire, as she felt the massive amount of liquid spewing from her pussy. But as the pressure that had built up relented, the monstrous orgasm it sparked left her unable to focus on anything other than the waves of pleasure inundating her body.

After collecting her spend, George put the pail aside. He was already hard again after watching Robyn's amazing display of liquified sexuality, thinking that this girl was incredible. But he decided to get her upstairs before screwing her again. Once he spun her around and saw the blank stare she gave him, he knew she was out of it, for now anyway. So, he hoisted her up, moved the table under her again, and then lowered her body onto it.

Robyn was not quite gone, as she kept mumbling, "Thank you Sir," over and over, but it was barely a whisper. George took his time unbinding her, slowly releasing each body part from its strict and debilitating confinement. The suspension left beautiful rope marks in her supple flesh, a sight that always pleased him. He chose to leave her hair connected to her anal hook, as he liked the idea of marching her upstairs with it tugging against her tail bone.

Robyn felt like a zombie. While she could feel how George was releasing her, and she was appreciative, she was so spent from her malicious deflowering that she no strength left to move at all. When he straightened her legs they cramped, and she groaned, but he massaged them until the muscles relaxed. It was like a dream, as she enjoyed the gentle way he released her from the cruel ropes encasing her body.

Robyn wondered when he would take the hook out of her asshole so she could relax her neck, but it never happened. She had somewhat regained her senses as he gradually unbound her, and when everything but the anal hook was removed, he dashed her hope that it would be too.

"Can you stand up slave?" he asked, now that she was lying on the table unfettered.

"Yes Sir," she reluctantly replied, her eyes still adjusting with the blindfold removed.

"Is that all you have to say?" he asked sternly.

"I'm sorry Sir! Thank you for taking my cherry! It was better than I ever imagined!" Robyn cried out, realizing she did owe him an enthusiastic thank you for sending her into sexual nirvana.

"Gratitude is the best gift a slave can give her Master. Would you like to call me Master now that I have shown you what it will be like to be my sex slave?"

"If it pleases you Sir, I would love to call you...Master," she replied in such a sweet voice that he almost considered unhooking her asshole.

"I will allow it, even though this is still a trial run. Now get up on your feet slave, we have more games to play tonight," he said.

"Yes Master," Robyn said, and she felt a massive thrill when she heard herself say it.

She was stiff, sore, and still light-headed from her airborne sexual jaunt, but she slid off of the table and onto her feet. Robyn had to lean against the table because her legs felt very weak. George moved against her body, pinning her back against the edge of the table. He held up the pail with one hand and dipped a finger into it with the other hand.

As he withdrew it, he said, "Taste your come slave," as he moved the wet finger toward her mouth.

"Yesss Massster," she cooed, just before she started sucking on the offered digit.

Robyn moaned contentedly as she suckled his finger, surprised that it tasted just like his cock did after he fucked her. She did not even know that women could ejaculate, but his bucket of girl come revealed another new and perfectly perverse addition to her sexual edification. As she stared up at him, Robyn felt like she actually belonged to him, and it made her tremble with renewed desire. Her sex was sore and sensitive, but she wanted more, and hoped his promised 'games' included plenty of sex!

When he withdrew his finger, he asked, "Are you ready to find out how many ways a man can fuck a slut?"

"Yesss Massster, please fuck your slave like the slut she is," Robyn purred, ready to jump his bones again. It was still hard to believe how she was feeling, something inside her had snapped, and she knew she was definitely a slut, and now she really wanted to be his slave! Because he made her feel like this, she believed that there was nothing she could deny him!

He marched her up to his room, with the hook in her ass relentlessly jerking against her sphincter and tail bone, further stirring up her saturated sex. By the time they reached his bedroom she was as wound up as she was just

176

before he took her in the dungeon playroom. Thankfully, before he began the next round of sexual frolicking, he removed the hook. The next thing she knew, Robyn was face down on his bed and he was on top of her. When his dick plunged back into her ravenous sex she screamed her thanks. For the next several hours Robyn got to find out what it was like to be tossed about and fucked like a sex toy, loving every minute of it. The only disappointing moment of the night came when, after he had fucked her in at least a dozen different positions, he ordered her into her 'comfy' cage and left her there to sleep alone. She was so spent that sleep came quickly, and her dreams were wonderful.

To be continued...

EPILOGUE

Robyn's real journey is just beginning and her story will be continued in the next part, 'Seduced Into Slavery.' While her first week of training was intense, becoming George's 24/7 slave trainee will become far more depraved. Now that George has 'deflowered' her and she has discovered how powerful kinky sex is with her potential Master, her motivation to explore her submission is stronger than ever. You are invited to join her on her quest along the strange and challenging path toward her total sexual submission. What started as an attempt to get into the pants of her handsome neighbor has become something she never imagined.

While she slept in her cage for the first time, her worries about why she was doing this were no longer her concern, as she basked in the glow of her first sexual tryst with her Master. But the next phase of her training, now that he opened the sexual floodgates, will stoke the fires inside her to the limits of human endurance. He will challenge her every sensibility, and fully expose the darkest depths of her own kinky soul. What will become of Robyn? Will she continue to embrace the ever increasing debauchery George plans for her? Or will she find a line she cannot cross and abandon her dream of being his sex slave?

Printed in Great Britain
by Amazon

19893862R00102